PERFECT
PRESCRIPTION

Carol Wood

CHIVERS

British Library Cataloguing in Publication Data available

This Large Print edition published by AudioGO Ltd, Bath, 2012.
Published by arrangement with the Author

U.K. Hardcover   ISBN   978 1 4713 1104 8
U.K. Softcover   ISBN   978 1 4713 1105 5

Printed and bound in Great Britain by
MPG Books Group Limited

CHAPTER ONE

Bruno . . . old English for brown if she wasn't much mistaken.

And in the few seconds Bruno Quillan had taken to hurtle past her like Halley's comet she'd certainly noticed the beautiful, rich, soil-brown eyes teased ever so subtly at the corners by very fine lines, like miniature fans opening up as he crinkled his gaze—though plainly enough not in her direction!

Then there was the hair. A thick, untidy sprawl of wavy dark brown over heavy, wide-set eyebrows—hair a woman would kill for and which, at present, as she stared at him across Reception, untidily irritated a collar made all the more uncomfortable by hooking a finger down it to jerk it out, allowing the deeply tanned throat a second's reprieve to breathe.

Dr Bruno Quillan, MD.

Frances blinked as for the first time the subject of her thoughts suddenly left his patient, turned on a sixpence and picked up speed, careering towards her right on collision course. Too late, she stepped back, and amidst the Monday morning mêlée somehow became attached to the eye of the cyclone. Papers and notes swirling through the air, she experienced the strange sensation of being weightless, then twirled until she was giddy, and finally and ignominiously being brought down to earth again—in a very strong pair of arms.

Breathless, and more than aware of a dozen pairs of eyes trained upon them, she steadied herself against the chest which was, she noticed irrelevantly, covered by a baggy sweater definitely not washed in a miracle powder as advertised on TV.

He said apologetically, setting her on her feet and bundling an assortment of papers back into her arms, 'Look . . . I really am sorry—hang on!'

Frances opened her mouth and closed it again as he whirled away, his attention stolen by one of the three Cherry Grove receptionists.

She stood obediently, clutching her armful of patient notes—once religiously arranged alphabetically, now in chaos.

'Hold on!' she heard him call again, and lifted her stricken gaze to see the broad shoulders overlapping petite little Suzie Collins in absorbed concentration.

Pulling her papers into a semblance of order and ignoring the smirks of one or two patients, she turned on her heel—perhaps he hadn't noticed before, but a nurse's time was precious too!

'Wait!' she heard again, and felt the warm tide of anger rise in her throat. He didn't even know her name. Hadn't bothered to ask. And probably, if he hadn't knocked her over, he

2

wouldn't even be aware of her existence now. Arrogant. Rude. And, by the looks of Suzie Collins' blushes, fancied himself a ladies' man.

Not turning around—indeed, increasing her pace—she found herself outside, where fresh air stormed into her lungs and tempered her angry cheeks, consoling herself with the thought that at least she could weather her six months with the other three doctors of the practice—all of whom had taken time to welcome her. Nigel Drew the senior partner had been particularly considerate, and had called the young Dr Tristan Keen in for a good hour-long consultation about their housebound patients; Even the brisk, cool, vivacious Meg Fellows had itemised the patients who she felt needed special care.

Was it only a fortnight ago that she'd transferred from London to Dorset? Frances wondered on an inner sigh, suddenly missing the city. Maybe she'd been mad to agree to cover for Benita Howarth, her friend, whilst she had her baby. Surely someone else would have volunteered? Still, what was six months? At the moment, Frances thought glumly, it seemed like a lifetime sentence on another planet.

'Ah . . . just a moment!'

Frances froze. So, he had followed her, had he? He might just as well be calling a dog to heel. Damn cheek. Who did he think he was?

She turned, chin up, casting him a withering

3

blue gaze and tossing back her long golden plait. The sun bounced off the modern glass-plated front of the practice building and for a moment blinded her, which rather spoiled the effect.

'Ah . . . sorry . . . again. Should have been more careful . . .'

She couldn't have agreed more! 'Next time I'll be a bit quicker,' she retorted, moving back a few inches to safety as he approached. 'And then you won't have the worry of accidentally steamrollering over a member of staff.'

The huge, languid, black-lashed eyes lit up. 'Ah . . . the lady has a sense of humour, I see!'

She narrowed her blue gaze. 'Fortunately, yes. And, much as it may surprise you, I also have a name.'

The unruly hair was suddenly disciplined by a large, solid hand sweeping it from his forehead, brown eyes the same shade glimmering with rueful amusement. 'Oh dear, I seem to have forgotten it for the moment—'

'For the moment?' She couldn't believe this. 'Dr Quillan, I arrived at this surgery a week ago!'

'A week, is it?'

'A week.'

'How remiss.' A faint, almost beguiling smile lifted the corners of his mouth. 'Brain like a sieve, I'm afraid.'

He thought that would wash, did he? 'We'd all like to be able to use that excuse,

4

Dr Quillan,' she intoned sweetly, 'but unfortunately it doesn't hold water.'

He roared with laughter, eyes lighting up. 'Brilliant!'

She could have kicked herself. 'It wasn't meant to be funny.'

He looked duly repentant, smothering his humour, which only made the lustre of brown in his eyes glow more deeply. 'Sorry. Really am. No excuses, just a miserably busy week.' One bushy eyebrow lifted. 'Forgive me?'

She drew herself up. 'It isn't a question of forgiveness. It's—'

'It's what? I mean, name-wise? I know you're our temporary DN, but I just haven't managed to catch your name. Truthfully, I haven't had a moment.'

Nor would he ever, she imagined! Doctors like Quillan were addicted to the rush of adrenalin, to being in demand, to being wanted and sought after and adored by patients and staff alike. Little tin gods. Just like Greg. Just like the man she was trying to forget. Correct that—the man she had forgotten. Almost. She sniffed. 'It's Duncan. Frances Duncan.'

He smiled. 'Frances? Good. Frances, yes. Ah . . . finding your feet, are you? You've met everyone, of course?'

'Except you,' she replied tightly, as heat irritatingly curled up her neck under the heavy-lidded brown gaze. 'But as I now seem to have your undivided attention, Dr Quillan, if you've a moment or two some time I'd appreciate a quick word about Frederick Clark. I made a fresh assessment of him this week and these are some of my notes—' she held them up by their entangled corners '—which I shall rearrange when I've a spare hour or two.'

The dark eyes glimmered with quiet amusement. 'So I'm not forgiven. The lady holds a grudge.'

'I do nothing of the kind!'

'Then have lunch with me today to prove you don't.'

'Lunch!' she spluttered, jaw dropping.

'Peace offering.'

Frances shook her head in wonderment. Two minutes ago he had been telling her his feet didn't touch the earth in his mission to save mankind, and now he was asking her out to lunch in the middle of a frantic Monday.

Wisely observing her horror, he slithered a few feet, raising the palms of his hands. 'OK, say no more. Message received and understood, Frances Duncan. Offer withdrawn.' He stuffed his curled palms into the deep pockets of baggy-legged, smooth-hipped corded trousers and grinned 'Now, tell me how I can help you with young Freddie? Would you like me to call?'

Self-consciously flicking back her thick hair, as smooth as gold and plaited into a straight, coiled tail which hung heavily down her spine, she nodded. 'It would put my mind at rest—though I can't actually say there's something amiss. Freddie's breastfed, but he seems discontent and sickly.'

'Sure. I'll check my visits when I come back this afternoon. Can you meet me back here at five?'

She licked dry lips. 'Fine. That will be perfect.'

He grinned 'How nice to hear I've done something right at last.' Then at her instant bristle he jumped away and loped off towards the car park. 'See you at five, Frances Duncan,' he called cheerfully, broad shoulders swaying under the sweater and the dark waves of his hair glinting chestnut as the sun sparked through it.

She watched him go, feeling stunned. Stunned either by the drift of limy aftershave filtering in his wake, or the realisation that her eyes were glued to the tall, rangy figure—not thin, but not large, just supple and tall and quick-moving, with long legs that sped him with a purposefulness to the Range Rover.

Strange man. Provoking man. And worse, sensual man. She wondered if he knew it and exploited it, and immediately snatched her eyes back as the Range Rover tooted and sped off.

A patient walked past her and she blinked.

Now, where was she?

Taking a deep breath, she glanced unsurely

back to Cerne Carey's Cherry Grove Health Centre. In London it would be warm and muggy with no breeze. Here the air was still, but clear, and there was a faint twang of pig manure. Greg had hated the country. He was a townie through and through. Where would he be now? she wondered, with a quick, sharp pang. Flying up the ranks probably. Unequivocally officer material. Would it have ever worked for them if she'd given it more time? Would he have ever asked her to marry him?

Both raised in army families—and with her training in the QAs, and Greg's career in the Royal Engineers as a bomb disposal expert— maybe she could have eventually convinced him. She wanted marriage and babies and convention, despite the modern swing towards partnerships. And she'd stuck out for it. Until the explosion in Ireland. He hadn't been killed, not that time. No, but there would be other times, and she'd seen enough injuries to know that a fatality was probably a merciful alternative to a life paralysed from head to foot.

If Greg had really loved her, he would have understood and married her. After all, there had been the suggestion from his CO that he take some leave and afterwards be reassigned. But no, the addiction was too strong, and that last night at the flat in London he'd told her he was going ahead with his posting to the Gulf . . . unless . . .'

'Fran?'

She jumped and whirled around to see Gillian Grant, one of the receptionists, hurrying to catch her up, pulling on an anorak as the sunny sky clouded over.

'Thrown in at the deep end this week, weren't you?' Gill chuckled as she hoisted her bag over her shoulder.

Too deep, Frances reflected bitterly, thinking that her induction might have been painless if one person in particular had stopped to discuss his patients with her, as the others had.

Still, no use moaning to Gill. 'Everyone's been very friendly.' She smiled, trying to erase the uncomfortable thought of the one who hadn't. 'Dr Drew and Dr Keen even shared their coffee-breaks with me.'

'And Meg Fellows? Now, she's a live-wire, isn't she?'

Frances laughed. 'Actually, Dr Fellows and I had an enthralling conversation on cheeses in the delicatessen the other day. She had a dinner party organised for that evening and we split the last of Mrs Dean's Camembert between us.' They both giggled, until Gill finally crooked a curious eyebrow. 'And what about Bruno Quillan?'

Frances grimaced. 'Don't ask.'

'Oh, take no notice of the Speed of Light!

That's what we call him, you know. Once you manage to pin him down, he's really very sweet. A workaholic, of course, but then he's had a lot to make him that way. I expect you know—' Gill suddenly stopped and waved at an estate car pulling in to the kerb. 'Oh, must go—there's my Keith. Turns purple if he has to wait five minutes for me or the kids. See you tomorrow, Fran.'

Frances watched her friend depart. The first delicate brush of May rain fell on her fair eyebrows and she knitted them thoughtfully. Gill was a lovely girl, always so bright and breezy. Of the three reception staff she'd been the most helpful, but not in a gossipy way. Frances wondered what she had been going to say about Bruno Quillan—still, whatever it was, she wasn't particularly interested. She knew enough about him already to have mentally, filed him under A for arrogant—and B for beyond belief. The other descriptions she had in mind at this moment defied all translation!

The rain pelted down and she ran to her little white Clio. The car had been a cheer-up pressie a year ago, from herself to herself After all, a girl needed a bit of a pick-me-up when she'd spent two years imagining she was the light of someone's life and then discovered she was little more than a twenty-five-watt bulb!

Smoothing back her fringe, she

determinedly shrugged off the depressing reminder and blinked hard at the 3D effect of the rain warring with the windscreen. Impulsively she switched on every knob she could see. Wipers, demister, stereo, side-lights.

Better. Yes.

Noise, colour—back into the land of the living.

Now, to the delicatessen, then home to the flat in Bow Lane to try to swot up on something that was worrying her about two-week-old Freddie Clark, because for sure, after their debacle today, Bruno Quillan would want more than just a sense of unease delivered to his busy doorstep.

In Cerne Carey's Delectable Delly, Frances brushed the rain from her dress and gazed at Mrs Dean's mouthwatering selections under the glass counters.

'Right-ho dear. Fire ahead,' Mrs Dean invited. And soon all the groceries were packed neatly into the recycled carrier bag. The shopkeeper took Frances's five-pound note then she stopped dead and frowned out of the window. 'Beggars again, is it? In all, this rain too!'

Frances followed her gaze. A rain-lashed pavement revealed a huddled figure leaning against the Clio, and Mrs Dean clucked. 'We had two last week playing guitars and blowing whistles. Whatever is the world coming to?'

But Frances's attention drifted as she

accepted her change. She grabbed her carrier and hurried out of the shop. Not beggars at all, but a boy!

As she approached one monster water droplet fell from his freckled nose and plopped onto the bonnet.

He wasn't more than nine or ten, she decided, and he was drenched to the skin.

'Can I help?' she shouted against the rain, and amidst a cacophony of wheezes she received the dubious information that he had missed a bus.

'Are you asthmatic?' she prodded to the dripping wet hood.

Two blue eyes blinked underneath, which she assumed meant yes.

Frances groaned inwardly. Nothing for it, she supposed, but to offer him a lift home. A lift he duly accepted, falling into the passenger seat like a sack of wet potatoes.

'My name's Frances,' she said, and handed over a tissue. 'What's yours?'

'J-ack . . .' she heard, and missed the rest as he blew and wheezed alternately. Finally she deciphered an address, one which luckily she knew since she'd had a patient last week in a house which backed on to Mayfield Crescent. Five minutes later she turned the Clio into a muddle of billowy rhododendrons lurching wetly across a sandy drive. At the end of it sat a big, square house. It was, she decided, like a huge pink birthday cake set in a great green wrapper.

'Is anyone in?' she asked, and could have kicked herself for not asking before as he shook his head.

'Do you have a key?' she persisted.

And to her relief he stabbed in his wet pocket and produced one. Relief which slowly darkened into dismay as once in the house, with his wet clothes discarded for a dressing gown, the wheezes refused to budge—despite the use of his inhaler.

Frances looked around the deserted kitchen. The Aga was stoically warm, and she pulled out a straight-backed chair from under the pine table. Shuffling it around, she gently drew the boy onto the seat, legs astride, with his elbows resting on the back to allow his chest muscles to force out air more efficiently.

'Now . . .' She smiled reassuringly as he strained for breath. 'I'll phone Mum or Dad. You do have a number where I can reach one of them, don't you?'

The blue eyes met with hers once more, huge and a wee bit sad—and strangely familiar. 'D-Dad's,' he stammered, and wheezed a number.

A number which Frances mentally logged in delayed shock, digested and then firmly rejected as impossible. She repeated it to him in a whisper, the hair standing up on the back of her neck as she gazed into the beautiful languid pools of cornflower-blue and turned

13

them into brown.

It couldn't be.

Fate surely wouldn't be so unkind.

But it was.

She hid her dismay as well as she could and went out into the hall to dial the number she already knew off by heart.

*   *   *

Bruno Quillan stared disbelievingly at his son.

Then, gently, he pulled the elastic of the nebuliser over the fair curly head and eased off the mask.

Jack Quillan took a hesitant, experimental breath.

'How is it now, Tiger?' His father tucked the collar of the dinosaur dressing gown softly under the wobbly chin.

'B-better,' Jack stammered.

Bruno smiled. 'Chest not so tight?'

A bleak nod and a sleepy blink of white-blond lashes as his father parted his pyjama top and listened to a skinny little chest through the Stethoscope.

Frances watched them, silent now after the panic of the last half-hour. She hardly knew if she was on her head or her heels. A week ago she hadn't known them, hadn't even set eyes on Jack, and yet in the space of a few hours she'd been propelled into what was obviously a full-scale family drama.

14

What were the odds that she should have discovered Bruno's son truanting from school? A million to one probably. And on today of all days, when she could have happily done without another contretemps with a certain doctor.

Obviously the same thought had struck Bruno Quillan when she'd rung him at Cherry Grove. 'My Jack?' he'd repeated incredulously. 'In the town centre? But he's at school. You must be mistaken.'

'I certainly am not!' she had snapped back, tired and damp and short on patience with this trying man. 'Do you think I've kidnapped someone else's child and brought him to your house?'

'Of course not . . .'

'Then are you coming home or shall I bring him in? Whichever way, it has to be quick.'

By the time she had convinced him and he had arrived Jack had deteriorated, and a nebuliser had had to be used to relieve the attack. His father had applied the measured dose of drugs and water into the reservoir and eased his son patiently into breathing the oxygen blown through the fluid.

Frances shivered in her damp dress.

'You're cold?' The tall man stared at her, his eyes running over the small-scaled delicacy of her figure, over the thin blue uniform dress and the way the rain had moulded it to her slender body. Before she could stop him he

15

vanished—as usual—and she was left alone with Jack, who gazed up at her from his warm. perch.

'Dad's going to be a-angry,' he stammered, and she wondered if the stammer was ingrained or if he was just upset.

'No, he won't be,' she reassured him gently. 'Not if you have a reason for being away from school, and I'm sure you have.'

'Will this do?' Bruno Quillan reappeared holding a sweater.

She felt suddenly embarrassed. 'It really doesn't matter . . .'

He held it up for her to put on. 'Nonsense. You'll catch pneumonia.'

Reluctantly she slipped in her arms, feeling his large body uncomfortably close behind her. No doubt his long-suffering wife was something of a knitter, she thought ruefully as she pushed back the sleeves and scooped out her damp plait.

'Warmer?'

She smiled for Jack's sake. He was looking at them curiously. 'What's happening at the surgery whilst you're here?' she asked, studiously avoiding the brown gaze.

'Oh, there's no problem. Tristan's covering for me. I'd pretty well finished for the morning anyway.' He seemed as though he was about to say something else, then decided better of it and instead looped a long arm around his son's shoulders and hauled him gently up.

16

'Come on, old chap, let's tuck you up on the sofa in the other room for a bit.'

Frances met Jack's eye and smiled. She watched the tiny figure move out of the kitchen, Bruno's large hand ruffling the head of blond waves. Now she wished she had paid more attention to Gill this morning. Not that she would have listened to gossip, but it would have been interesting to know a little more of this family's background.

She stared around, looking for clues. The place was sprinkled with dishes and packets and memos pinned to cork boards, and a happy pile of rubbish grew out of the open drawer of an old pine dresser. Mrs Quillan hadn't tidied today—maybe she had a hairdresser's appointment or a coffee afternoon arranging charitable events with other deserted wives?

Hearing footsteps along the hall, she turned back and the man himself appeared, large and dishevelled, his presence seeming to fill the kitchen. 'I'm sorry I took a bit of convincing when you phoned. It just didn't seem very likely.'

'Meaning I went deliberately out of my way to discover your son and drag him back here just to embarrass you?' she asked on an affronted gasp.

'No, not that at all.' He shrugged. 'I wasn't the least embarrassed. Just surprised. And it took a few moments to jell.'

Suppressing her desire to comment that no one had been more surprised than she on discovering Jack's parentage, she picked up the Ventolin inhaler from the table and decided to change the subject. 'This was no use at all, I'm afraid. How often is he having these attacks?'

He took it from her, fingers brushing hers for a second, and she flinched, letting go as though she'd had an electric shock. Had he seen the reaction? she wondered, and was furious with herself as he smiled briefly, the faintest hint of amusement flaring in the depths of his eyes before they wandered purposefully over the rest of her face and came to rest on the open surprise of her full mouth.

'Several of late—although previous to those he was doing pretty well. Hence the nebuliser. I keep this one here at home in case of emergencies—not that we've had call to use it until now. What concerns me is why he skipped school and why he didn't ring me to come and pick him up.'

Something warned her that the water was far deeper here at the Quillan household than at the surgery, and that was bad enough. 'I'm afraid he didn't say.' She shrugged. 'But I'm sure he'll tell you in his own good time, or Mum will prise it out of him eventually.'

The expression on his face changed and he stiffened, wandering over to the big bay window, and with a start she realised that dark

18

hollows had suddenly engraved themselves under his eyes as he stared out. 'I only wish it were so. I'm afraid Lindsay, Jack's mother, died when he was four.'

Oh, idiot! she thought helplessly. She hadn't even considered the possibility of Jack being motherless, and yet shouldn't she have? After all, Jack would have said something about his mum if she were alive, wouldn't he? 'I'm sorry,' she apologised softly. 'I didn't know.'

'Again . . . I'm surprised.' He turned from the window and he caught her off guard with the remark.

'Surprised I didn't know?' she said bewilderedly.

'Well . . . it is common enough knowledge. There's bound to be gossip amongst the staff—'

'If you think your staff have time for prurient gossip, Dr Quillan,' she cut in sharply, 'you're very much mistaken. No one has said anything about you or Jack's mother—and why should they? I certainly haven't asked!'

He gave her a strange look. 'You are a fiery little thing, Frances Duncan. Is it just me you react to like this, or do you have a poor opinion of men in general?'

Her mouth fell open. 'That's ridiculous!'

He arched dark, very disbelieving eyebrows. 'Is it, indeed?'

'How—how dare you suggest . . .?'

Suddenly he laughed, and caught her so

unawares with the sound that she fully forgot what she was going to say. And then she made the mistake of glaring into the crinkly brown eyes, and she just stood there; like an imbecile, mesmerised by the intimacy of the expression that seemed to emanate from them and spread over her like a deliciously soft veil of silk.

'I wasn't suggesting anything,' he said with a shrug as his mirth died. 'I suppose I wanted a reaction and I got one. It's—ah—just something about you, I'm afraid. Something about those little drawn back shoulders and sparkling blue eyes which tempts me to—'

'Well, please avoid the temptation in future,' she snapped, trying to recover and utterly confused by the trembling which seemed to be communicating itself from limb to limb. She pulled the sweater around her as if for protection. 'I must go.'

He stepped forward into her path, and she stopped so abruptly that she felt her teeth snap together. 'Whoa, there . . . slow down!'

She thrust out her chin and glared fiercely at him. 'I don't intend to stay and be ridiculed—'

'And I have no intention of ridiculing.' He looked down at her with genuine concern. 'Listen, can we start again? You obviously did us a great service today. I want to thank you, not alienate you. And I know Jack's grandmother would be furious with me if I let you go on a misunderstanding.'

Frances hesitated, her curiosity suddenly

prevailing over her anger. 'Jack's grand-mother?'

He nodded. 'I cope only with her wonderful help. Rosa happens to be away this week, visiting a friend in the Lakes. Maybe, this has something to do with Jack's truancy, although I can't think what. I rang the school just now. They have no idea why he disappeared.'

Frances was at a loss to comment. Obviously something had upset the child, and pretty badly too. 'Well, I'm afraid I haven't either.' She sighed deeply. 'He said barely a word. Anyway . . . I really must go. Say goodbye to Jack for me. I won't disturb him again.'

He nodded and opened the kitchen door wider, and as she passed her eyes caught the unbuttoned shirt and the deep brown, vulnerable well of exposed throat beneath, provoking a strange sensation inside her like a bird fluttering, caught in her ribs. A chill, she thought logically, dragging her eyes back to the hall. Two paracetamol when you get home, my girl.

'I shan't be going back to Cherry Grove,' he said as he followed her to the front door. 'It's Freddie Clark you're concerned about, isn't it?'

She hesitated for a moment as the thought of the grizzling baby crossed her mind, but in view of Jack she put it to one side. 'It can wait, I suppose. There's nothing I can actually put my finger on anyway . . .'

21

'Why hasn't Freddie's mother asked for a call?'

She shrugged. 'Mrs Clark doesn't want to make a fuss—she says. Thinks it's probably the usual problems with breast-feeding. But all the same I'd rather you check. I did try to talk to you last week, when she first came home with him from hospital, but you weren't available.'

'I'll go tomorrow.' He stuck his hand in his hair, abstractedly drawing it through the thick brown waves, and in the brightness of day she saw the lines of tension beading his brow. For a moment she wondered what had made her react so violently against him—not that sympathy had soothed her anger. All she had waited for last week was acknowledgement, a common courtesy and a spared quarter of an hour in which they could have discussed patients like Sarah Clark and Freddie to give her some idea of what to expect when she visited them. Instead, he had whistled around the practice like a gale-force wind—and ignored her. It was hard to believe the slight was deliberate. If it wasn't, then it was just downright rude!

'Come with me if you like,' he suggested suddenly.

She was startled. 'To see Freddie? But what about Jack? Do you think he'll be well enough for school?'

'I don't know. I'll just have to play it by ear. If he's well. I'll go into school with him and have a word with the headmaster.'

Suddenly a thin, yawning voice asked, 'Is Fran going?'

Bruno grinned as a pale figure came along the hall. It nudged against his hip and he wrapped his fingers under the upturned chin. 'It's Sister Duncan, Jack.'

Frances laughed. 'Heavens no. We got our heads around that one hours ago, didn't we, Jack? Fran's fine.'

Jack giggled. 'Bye, Fran.'

She had the impossible urge to bend and hug him. But she didn't, of course, and found herself hurrying away, drawing the warmth of the sweater around her.

She turned back as she got to the car. Her new employer stood with his son, one large hand resting on a narrow shoulder. Father's eyes were son's eyes—large, expressive and soulful. Though one set was blue and the other brown. And both sets of eyes, for one moment, locked with her own.

She took a deep breath as she sunk into the Clio's soft seat and wound down the window. 'Take care, Jack,' she called. Starting the engine, she drove away without glancing in her rear mirror—though she had the weirdest sensation that Bruno Quillan would be watching her car until it disappeared from sight.

*   *   *

Frances glanced at the wall-clock and expelled a breath. Half-seven!

She slid out of the shower and glanced around the cosy little mews flat she had leased in Bow Lane. Dried flowers and pot-pourri now brightened the corners and she'd hung one or two brasses on the beams just to make it feel like home whilst she was here. Her own flat in north-west one was safely locked and regularly checked by the caretaker. Six months away from London . . . This morning it seemed even further away than yesterday . . .

As she towel-dried herself her hair, set free from its band, fell in a golden shower as she bent over, stepping into soft lacy briefs and sliding a white silk camisole over her bra. The phone rang and she groaned. 'Frances Duncan,' she sighed, after grabbing it, wriggling into her clean dress at the same time.

'Frances? Have I caught you at a bad moment?'

Bruno Quillan! She regarded herself despairingly in the mirror. 'No,' she lied brightly, 'not at all. How is Jack?'

'I'm leaving with him for school. I wondered, as I'm on my way in through town, can you meet me at the Clarks'? I should make it about nine-fifteen.'

She'd have to get a move on, but she couldn't miss this opportunity. 'All right. See you there.' She paused. 'Tell Jack I said hi.'

'Tell him yourself, if you like.'

There came a rummaging sound and a slightly wheezy hello.

'Feeling better?'

'A bit.'

'Well, no abseiling or sky-diving for at least twelve hours! Nurse's orders.'

Laughter came over the phone and she was glad. Then with a bit of a cough he mumbled, 'I'd better go. See you, Fran.'

She called goodbye and replaced the receiver slowly, with an odd little pang in her heart—one which she told herself was not hers to have. After all, how long had she known the child? Besides, lots of kids had asthma when they were young, and he'd probably grow out of it. Despite her mental reassurances, though, as she went on getting dressed she still thought about him. Had his father managed to find out the reason for his truancy?

It was fifteen minutes more before she managed to finish.

Early summer brought with it the advantage of wearing as little as possible under her dark blue cotton uniform. Her petite five-five figure required no tights. Her legs were smoothly brown from the early Easter sunshine and the tiny bit of sunbathing she'd managed in London, squeezed in on the lounger of her flat's roof garden.

Bruno was already at the Clarks' when she arrived. She parked the Clio behind the racing-

25

green Range Rover and noticed that there was at least an inch-thick crust of mud across the bumper and wheel arches which matched the film on the Clio—obviously from the sandy drive of the pink house.

'You look drier this morning.' He grinned as he met her on the pavement. This morning there was no trace of the open neck of yesterday. A blue tie sat squarely on the broad chest and a matching blue shirt with just a few tell-tale creases lurking at the shoulders drew her eyes to the pectoral muscle beneath, moving like rock under sea water, she thought—and tried to stop thinking.

'What kind of a reception did you have at school?' she asked as he pushed open the Clarks' front gate for her.

He shrugged. 'Drew a blank. Jack's been OK up until this week. I didn't manage to get a thing from him last night and I didn't want to push it. He seemed happy enough to go in this morning. Bit of a cold looming, I think.'

Frances wasn't in the least surprised. She expected one herself 'Perhaps it will all blow over,' she said, and realised that she'd made another pun.

He laughed, the brown eyes crinkling up as he stared at her with that strange mixture of amusement and attraction. 'Perhaps it will, Frances Duncan,' he agreed gently.

She glanced up into the smooth oily pools and felt that weird little flutter under her ribs.

She blushed and looked away, then licked her lips. 'Ah . . . I haven't much to tell you about Freddie, I'm afraid, except that I would have thought the vomiting might have lessened by now.'

He jabbed a finger on the bell-push. 'Does it interfere with his feeding?'

'No . . . not that Mum has mentioned.'

The door opened and a dark-haired young woman carrying a baby in her arms stared at them in surprise. Bruno Quillan was quick to explain that he was assimilating his cases with Frances, and asked if she would consider sparing them a few moments. Frances registered a slight hesitation, but Sarah let them in, and very soon little Freddie, who had just been fed, lay on a soft bathing mattress and exercised his young lungs.

'How's his weight?' Bruno asked, checking the tiny heartbeat and pinkly thrashing limbs.

The baby's mother shrugged dismissively. 'Well . . . he lost it, of course, at first—like they all do. But the midwife seemed happy enough with it.'

Bruno nodded as the starfish fingers gripped his thumb. 'Good. How are your nights going?'

Sarah sighed. 'Terrible. But I suppose I'm coping.'

'In what way terrible?' Bruno asked gently.

'Oh, nothing, really. I was just spoilt with Joanna, I suppose. She was a dream. At two weeks she always slept through till six.'

Bruno smiled. 'A mixed blessing, perhaps.'

Just then the baby hiccuped. Frances noticed that he had been sick on Sarah's dress, and tactfully dabbed at it with a tissue.

'He is a bit sickly,' Sarah said quickly. 'But then so was Joanna. I expect my milk's a bit rich.'

Bruno clipped his case closed. 'His stools are normal?'

She nodded, glancing back at Frances. 'You're . . . you're not worried about anything, are you? I mean, he's well, isn't he?'

Bruno smiled reassuringly. 'He's a healthy little chap. Apart from the regurgitation of milk, he's fine. But with sickness—in fact with anything unusual or out of the way—we like to keep an eye.'

Sarah Clark hesitated. 'Will you call again?'

Frances nodded. 'I'll come at the end of the week.'

Surprisingly the young woman didn't show much enthusiasm, and Frances wondered if it was because they had called without phoning first. New babies were always a handful, and having someone appear on the doorstep might be a bit disconcerting. She said as much to Bruno as they stood outside on the pavement by the Range Rover.

'Perhaps I'm imagining it,' Frances said with a sigh as she glanced back at the house, 'but I felt Sarah was uptight. I've seen her three

28

times since she came home from hospital, and each time I feel she's withdrawing a little.'

Bruno hesitated as he angled his key towards the lock. 'Postnatal depression?'

'Possibly . . .'

'And the baby is picking it up—hence the sickness?'

Frances saw a movement from behind the net curtains. 'Better go. Shall I see you back at the surgery?'

His eye, too, seemed drawn back to the house. 'Er . . . yes. Make it before three. I'll be leaving then to collect Jack.'

'Of course—you're single-handed this week, aren't you?'

He raised his eyes heavenward as he clambered into the Range Rover. 'Tell me about it!'

Before she could think carefully, and for some unfathomable reason, she said impetuously, 'I'll collect Jack, if you like. It's Cerne Carey Primary, isn't it? I've a call to make at the almshouses just beside it.'

He frowned down at her, his large body half in and half out of the Range Rover. 'Are you sure?'

She realised that it was too late to backtrack. Why on earth had she offered like that? The last thing she wanted was to seem to be ingratiating herself with a man like Bruno Quillan. 'It's no trouble. And, well, I suppose . . . if you're happy to leave him with me, he

29

could come home for tea.'

He stared at her for a moment, and she suddenly thought, What on earth am I saying? She was digging herself into an enormous hole and sinking deeper with everything she said!

He gave her a wide smile. 'OK, then. If you're sure—I'll ring school and let them know you're coming.'

She ducked back to the car in a flush of heat. What have you done? What have you said? she wailed, inside. Another voice called back immediately, rationally, You're just being considerate after yesterday because you like the boy—and because . . . Because what?

Well, she was just being helpful, wasn't she?

There was no ulterior motive in occupying Jack for a couple of hours and then returning him safely home—was there? She would do the same for anyone.

Frances caught her innocent blue eyes in the mirror and knew that she was fibbing to herself. Fibbing hugely. And she snapped them away from her reflection before she saw a more truthful answer written in them.

CHAPTER TWO

Gabriel Bally was Frances's gastrointestinal patient of forty-nine. He was an architect, holding down a high-pressured job, and he'd struck Frances, on the one occasion she'd met him during her first week, as a patient who was particularly prone to anxiety.

Benita had written copious notes in his care-plan, but nevertheless Frances was concerned. He had had little if any improvement in his stomach complaints, and he was just home from an oesophagoscopy when she arrived at the house. His young wife politely but firmly asked Frances to call the followings week, saying that he was asleep.

Frances wondered as she drove away from their luxurious home whether her next patient—a housebound pensioner—would prove as reluctant to see her as Gabriel Bally and Sarah Clark. Bruno Quillan could have helped her here, as they, were his patients—if he had deigned to give her some of his time, she might have had better success.

Luckily, pensioner Cynthia Vail, after some initial hesitation at being confronted with Benita's absence and first refusing to allow Frances in, posed less of a problem as she talked to her in depth about the importance of a nutritional diet. As Cynthia lived in one of the almshouses next to the school she spent rather longer with her than she would have normally, and Jack was waiting for her when she arrived at the school gates.

He climbed into the Clio with wide blue eyes and a rucksack bulging with books. 'Am I coming on your calls with you?' he asked, and

Frances laughed as she stowed the luggage on the back seat.

'No, I'm all finished. I rang my last patients and asked them if they wouldn't mind me calling tomorrow.'

'Won't you get into trouble?'

She slid the gear into second and turned the car towards Bow Lane, glancing back at him in surprise. 'What makes you think that?'

Jack looked thoughtful. 'I suppose being a nurse is not so strict as being a doctor.'

Frances smiled. 'Well . . . being a doctor is a very responsible job—'

'Especially if you're a fund-holder,' Jack interrupted her, sounding very worldly. 'Dad wasn't once and now he is, and that means he has to work twice as hard. Grandma says we have to appreciate the time we do spend together and make the most of it.'

The little chin stuck out and her heart constricted. She realised that in their short acquaintance she had learned a lot. Jack was obviously painfully aware of the attention he received, either from his grandmother or Bruno. He knew the score. He even talked like a grown-up sometimes. But just below the surface, in those evocative blue eyes, she saw something so childishly vulnerable that it hurt, and she had the sudden and dangerous urge to protect.

She shouldn't. He had a grandmother and a father who loved him, yet, none the less, the

32

question nagged her. How much time did the busy Dr Quillan allot to his family? If it was as much or as little as he gave his staff . . .

Stop it, she told herself angrily. The Quillans were none of her business. She was simply doing her good deed for the day, or that was what she told herself—what one half of her wanted to believe. She wasn't going to listen to the other half!

* * *

They ate pasta and chocolate-covered mousse and Jack chattered on about his computer at home. Then they played Cluedo, and Jack was Miss Scarlet, which he thought hilarious, and managed to get into the murder room in two throws.

As the warm May sun waned behind the chimneyed skyline of the mews in Bow Lane Frances glanced at her watch, surprised at the hour. 'Eight o'clock, Jack.'

He drew a small hand over his eyes. 'D-do I have to go?' It was the first time he'd stuttered. Frances had quite forgotten both the asthma and the stutter.

'We had better. I promised your father at the latest eight.'

'But Dad p-probably won't be home and Grandma's not there.' He stammered again. The speech impediment made an appearance, she reflected, when he was agitated.

'If he's not, I'll stay with you,' she said, and quickly added, 'You can show me this famous computer, perhaps?'

His face brightened and she dug her hands thoughtfully into her jeans pockets. Lots of children had stammers, and asthma too—sometimes brought on by stress and sometimes by allergies. There could be any amount of reasons for an attack of either, but up to now, whilst he had been happily occupied, neither had troubled him.

She gazed down affectionately at the tiny figure . . . small for ten. He looked more like eight, and not at all Bruno's build. He'd brought his jeans from his locker in school and they both wore T-shirts—Jack's white and hers a blue-grey, matching her eyes. Her long fair hair was a shade more ashen than Jack's, and hers was straight and thick whereas his was soft and wavy. With a shock she caught their reflection in the minor. They could almost be related—same colouring, same hair, same small build. What, then, had Lindsay Quillan looked like? Something like her? she wondered curiously.

The boy gathered his belongings and stood quietly at the door while Frances fished in her bag for her keys. Amazingly, not once during the evening had her thoughts drifted to Greg.

*　　　*　　　*

Jack was right. Bruno wasn't at home. The pink house looked lost and forlorn in the warm dusk, but the gardens smelt wonderful and the porch suffused the air with fragrant honeysuckle. Jack dug out the proverbial key and, to her dismay, began to wheeze.

They switched on the lights and Frances made a cool drink whilst Jack went upstairs to take his medication and get washed and changed. When he came down he didn't seem keen to show her his beloved computer, so she suggested they read.

At nine his father burst in, dark shadow around his jaw, tousled hair flicking about his collar—a collar still as yet closed by a tie, until, staring at them on the settee, he tugged at it with a groan. 'Lord . . . I'm sorry! What on earth is the time?'

Frances stared up from where she'd been nestled next to Jack on the sofa, glued to *King Solomon's Mines*. 'I haven't an earthly, actually. It doesn't matter. We've been lost in a book.'

'But I promised eight—'

'It really doesn't matter . . .' She closed the book and put her bare feet down on the floor.

Concerned brown eyes went down to Jack. 'How did it go today, Tiger?'

Jack rubbed his eyes and Frances realised that he was very tired. The bronchodilator he had used earlier had stopped the onset of the asthma, yet he did sound a bit chesty still though perhaps now that his father was home he would settle down.

He yawned massively. 'I won at Cluedo,' he grinned.

Looking relieved, Bruno sank down in a chair. 'Lord, it's ages since I played that game.'

'And Fran's got a nice flat,' Jack mumbled, and touched Frances's gaze with his own, like a small, unspoken message of approval. Then he yawned so widely that Bruno said he thought it was about time for bed, and Frances shot up and almost sprinted to the door.

'Stay and have coffee,' her host offered politely. 'At least I can offer you a drink after all you've done for us.'

She shook her head. 'No. I shan't—thanks all the same. It's late and I've a few notes I want to look at before tomorrow.'

'Glutton for punishment?' He looked at her wryly. 'Well, let me at least see you to the car. Jack, you go on up and I'll be there shortly.'

'Night, Fran.' The child peeled himself upward. He stood in front of her, lost in his voluminous dressing gown. She went to bend down, her spontaneous reaction to plant a kiss on his cheek, and then she realised that it was probably the last thing he wanted her to do. So she cracked a joke and got him giggling, and then watched the scurrying of carpet slippers up the stairs.

Unbidden, the pinch of muscle inside her ribs came again, and she swallowed, dragging up her bag from a chair and heading for the front door: She was aware of an arm jerking it open for her. The soft, scent-filled night soothed all her scattered senses a little, and she slowed down as she discovered Bruno walking beside her, hands thrust deeply into pockets.

'Please . . . go to Jack,' she said, and stopped. 'I can see myself out.'

'There's a bend in the drive that's awkward in twilight,' he told her, and walked on. 'I'll just see you safely through.'

She was glad, in the dusk, that he couldn't see her properly. All she wanted was to get as far away as possible now he was home. In fact, she felt slightly guilty, and she didn't know why. Possibly because she had been in his home? With his son? And he hadn't asked her, not really. She could have dropped Jack back to the surgery and let him cope yesterday . . .

At the car, she scraped her keys from her bag. 'Goodnight, then. See you tomorrow,' she mumbled, acute embarrassment for some reason making her ridiculously flustered.

'Frances?' He laid a hand on her door, which effectively stopped her from opening it.

She stared up at him, her heart beating savagely, but she commanded it to quieten, which it did—until she focused on the white teeth glimmering in the darkness, and then all her calmness went and she felt her body shiver convulsively. 'Y-yes?'

'Sorry about tonight. I'm outrageously late. And Jack sounds wheezy again.'

She paused a second. 'What time you come home is entirely your business, not mine—'

'You don't mean that at all,' he corrected her quietly. 'You mean it was because I wasn't here and the house was deserted that Jack became anxious. God knows—' he sighed heavily, leaning against the car '—I haven't even coped a day without Rosa. I didn't realise how much we'd miss her.' His shoulders seemed to droop as he added in an even quieter tone, 'I had a call, you see, just as I was coming home. An old chap with carcinoma of the liver. He died shortly after I arrived there.'

Suddenly she felt a pang of sympathy for him. It must be intolerable sometimes—parent versus doctor, priorities inextricably opposed. From somewhere above an owl made that curious, summer sound of nightly vigil, and it seemed to Frances to echo in the stars and moonlit sky, and between the flowers and the small, humming, tireless garden insects . . . and in, her own heart, like a fragile, whispering spirit.

As though it was the most natural thing in the world, the dark figure lifted itself from her car and reached out, taking her hands in his own, and she found herself, almost in slow motion, being taken into the warm circle of his arms She felt the strange and tentative breath on her cheek of a man whom she hardly knew

38

but felt she had known a lifetime, and was suddenly lost, drenched, drowned in sensation as he bent to kiss her, fully on the mouth.

Not that it lasted terribly long, she realised later.

Fingers brushed her cheek all too quickly as she opened her eyes and gazed into the face shadowed by moonlight. She felt his deep sigh under her breasts, and the slow stiffening of his body. Her lips were on fire, and she drew the tip of her tongue across them just to check to see if she could feel where his mouth had been. Her heart beat so rapidly that she swallowed as the pulse in her ears drummed a crazy course towards her brain.

He said, still with his arms around her, 'You're so lovely, so sweet . . .'

She blinked, wondering what she had done. What he had done. And to her shocked disbelief she found that she had allowed him to do it! For one brief second he touched her hair.

She started away from him then, realising what had happened with a horror that filled her bones and brought them to snap back in erect attention. She could hardly believe what had happened. She stared in disbelief at his outline, just making out the firm ridge of jaw, remembering inconsequentially the prickle of his stubble on her skin as he had kissed her.

He said huskily, 'If you stand there for very much longer looking at me like that, I just might not be responsible for my actions. You'd better go.' He gave a soft groan, as though he were about to take her in his arms again, and she moved back, the touch of the cold metal of the Clio on her arm suddenly bringing her back to reality.

Before she knew what she was doing, she'd pulled open the door and jumped in, fumbling with the starter until it burst into life. The Clio leap-frogged into action and, not daring to look out of the window or in her mirror as a figure loomed on the periphery of her vision, she picked up speed and soared down the sandy drive.

She drove out onto the main road, forced herself to concentrate until she navigated Cerne Carey town centre, and then finally entered Bow Lane and stopped the car with a jerk that almost sent her head springing off her neck. She unclipped her seat belt and spread her numbed fingers over her face.

She didn't even like the man and yet she had let him kiss her . . . And heaven forbid . . . had she kissed him back? Surely not?

As she wound down her window she gulped at the air and held up her face to the soft summer breeze. And then she remembered it. Every single breath and nuance, the soft, gentle pressure of lips and then the heady entry of a smooth, sweet tongue as she'd opened her mouth and it had flicked so sensually over her teeth.

Oh, no. Oh, yes.

Yes.

It was Tristan Keen who announced Bruno's absence from the surgery the following day.

'I'm taking all of Bruno's list this morning,' he told Penny Orchard, one of the part-time receptionists. 'And Nigel is doing the afternoons. Anyone who wants to see Bruno specifically had better be told to come next week.'

Hearing the young doctor, Frances looked up from the computer where she was sitting, and in between the four or five bodies crowding the reception area she saw Penny reach to remove Bruno's nameplate and insert Tristan's.

Penny looked harassed. She caught Frances's eye and shrugged. Frances got up from her seat, failed to catch Tristan before he leapt away and only managed to corner Nigel Drew the senior partner as he scooted through, head down, to the car park.

'Bruno's due a few days' leave from Christmas,' Nigel told her, ruffling his grey thatch of hair with a Biro. 'If you're really worried about a domiciliary, put it in the book and I'll try to find time later.'

Frances was left with a sinking feeling Perhaps Jack's cold had developed? Without Rosa, Bruno would have to remain at home. On the other hand, what if it was not to do with Jack, but with what had happened

41

between them last night?

Why, oh, why had she let him kiss her? So foolish! Their relationship was already daggers drawn, and yet, to complicate matters more, he had made that pass and she had let him. Why, after all those months of thinking of Greg, had she let a perfect stranger do that? And then it suddenly clicked. She was still on the rebound, obviously, from Greg. Apart from which, she was probably lonely—missing London, her friends, the busy city practice.

Comforting herself with a rational conclusion to a very irrational happening, she was left with the certainty that last night had been a colossal mistake. And damn the man for making her make it. Now it was embarrassment all ways round. One heady May evening and a whole six months ahead of her trying to pretend it hadn't happened.

The morning and the afternoon merged dully as Frances completed her calls—seven in all for that day. Most of them were straightforward, post-op cases, and there was a man who'd had an op for tenosynovitis—a severe inflammation of a tendon in his hand causing acute pain. The simple operation had followed an unsuccessful course of steroid treatment. Eventually the thirty-eight-year-old builder had decided to have a simple surgical slit to open the constricting synovium, allowing the tendon to move freely again.

'Bit messy, is it?' Richard Grove frowned as

she examined the wound and redressed it.

She shook her head, seeing nothing untoward. 'When's your follow-up appointment?' she asked as the man impatiently tried to wiggle his index finger.

'Next week. Can't come too soon.'

She hesitated. 'You'll have to be careful. The point is to keep it free from infection. No going back to work too soon.'

The builder groaned. 'I'm self-employed. No one's going to pay my bills for me. As I told Bruno Quillan last time, the boy's private schooling costs a bundle. Not that the professional classes have to worry. He won't bat an eyelid at the fees.'

Frances looked up. 'But Dr Quillan's son attends Cerne Carey Primary.'

Richard Grove studied her with interest. 'Soon won't be, if I'm any judge of character. Why should a doctor's son have to mix with the working classes? I mean, if a builder like me can get away with private education, why shouldn't he?'

Frances bit back her curiosity and packed away her case whilst her disgruntled patient continued to put the world to rights—though he made no further comment on Bruno. She supposed that they must know each other well for the man to suggest what he had about private education.

Stop it, Frances Duncan, she told herself as she drove to Bow Lane. Stop thinking about the Quillans. But as she prepared for her session of squash at the sports centre with a nursing colleague her mind kept playing a video, picking at scenes, bringing up that fateful kiss into full focus.

She half expected a call in the evening when she got home. She still had his sweater, she thought suddenly—as if that meant anything!

*   *   *

He didn't show up for work on Thursday, or Friday either. And over the weekend she was convinced beyond any doubt that he was more of an arrogant opportunist than she'd believed at first. What decent human being wouldn't at least ring up to say he was sorry about what had happened? She was a new member of staff—he'd ignored her all the first week and then made a pass in the second! Unbelievable!

The only reason she wasn't blowing steam out of her ears was Jack. He was a lovely child, unaffected and sensitive, and she'd felt drawn instinctively towards helping him But that way lay foolishness. For how could she allow herself to grow fond of the child when he had Bruno Quillan for a father?

Absent-mindedly pressing the warm, thick green wool of the sweater into her face and inhaling the lemony-lime scent from its fibres, she sighed. What a mess!

44

Oddly, in the first few seconds of seeing him, she didn't fall prey to spontaneous combustion. Which was what she'd thought she'd probably do. Instead, she felt calm and lucid. Did he really think he could treat her so shamefully and get away with it? True, as she saw him climbing out of the Range Rover she moved away from the office window and leant back on the cold wall and took her breath. True, her heart had taken a high jump and seemed to be lodged somewhere in her throat. But, disregarding all the physical symptoms manifested by anger, she determined to play it cool. As cool as he had anyway.

He wouldn't, she was sure, come into the office where she was. A hundred and one questions awaited him on a busy Monday morning in Reception.

She was wrong. He came in, brown eyes flashing up to meet hers. 'Frances . . .?'

'Good morning, Dr Quillan.' She was businesslike, her shoulders pulled back, her chin up, and she was holding someone's records. She was functional. Just.

He closed the door, a large hand coming up, as she had known it would, to sweep the thick brown wave from his forehead. 'Frances, I—'

'How's Jack?' She had managed, thank God, to string two plausible words together.

'A few ups and downs. He'll survive.'

45

She nodded, aware that she'd run out of questions and that the dangerous spark of anger was creeping into a full flush on her cheeks.

'Frances, I need to talk to you.'

'Is Rosa home?'

He gave a small jerk of his head. 'Yes, she's back. Frances, I wanted to ring you . . .' He walked towards her. 'When can we talk?'

She snatched the records into her waist. 'No! I mean . . . whatever it is you want to say, you can say it here.'

He looked surprised. 'Are you prepared to take that chance?'

She gaped at him. 'I don't know what you mean!'

'Don't you?' He raised his brows as her expression froze. 'Oh, come now, I think you do.'

'Dr Quillan—'

He leant towards her, asking softly, 'Come to the house tonight?'

'And why should I do that?' she gasped. 'Why should I be so foolish as to expose myself again to the kind of behaviour I wouldn't expect from an adolescent?' Damn, she hadn't meant to refer to it. It was up to him to apologise, not make her squirm like this.

'And who was the adolescent—you or me?'

She wanted to throw something at him, but patient notes were too precious. 'That's a terrible thing to say! You know exactly what

46

you did—'

'And the woman I did it to hardly leapt out of my arms. I had the distinct impression she was enjoying herself too much to complain.'

Her heart sank at the accusation, but it was saved from sinking irretrievably as her anger flooded back like a tidal wave. 'I wasn't given the opportunity to register it! Now, if you'll excuse me—'

He stood in her path as she tried to open the door. 'No, I shan't excuse you. Not until you agree to talk to me.'

'I have—and it's got us precisely nowhere!'

He shrugged. 'I wouldn't say that. I think we've already solved one or two minor issues.'

She inhaled a breath. Will you please stop—?' She caught her breath as the door flew open.

Nigel Drew poked his head in and stared at them, his eyes seeming to fall first on her flushed cheeks and glistening blue eyes. Then he switched to Bruno and growled, 'Here you are, man! I've been looking everywhere. I've one of your patients with me. Can you come?'

Bruno nodded, gave her one last amused glance, then turned and ambled out of the room, leaving her with her mouth agape and Nigel staring at her curiously. That was all she needed, she thought miserably, just managing to pull herself together. To achieve for herself a reputation in under a month was pretty good going on the whole, and that was what she would do if she was found like this again—on her own with Bruno Quillan, the air as electric as a thunderstorm.

It was too late for her to say anything. Nigel dashed away and she heard Gill Grant and Penny Orchard both needing signatures outside, and Bruno's deep voice in response.

'Dr Quillan, you've two emergencies on the trot and we're half an hour behind,' said Gill, and then the door swung closed and she was left in silence again.

The cheek of the man! She could hardly believe it. Angrily she thrust the patient notes back into the carousel, and then, waiting until it sounded quieter outside, and not looking either way as she hurried out, managed to make an exit from the practice.

After lunch at the flat and a simmering down which she achieved only by a concerted effort and a bowl of fruit cocktail liberally and naughtily laced with fresh cream, she called at Madjur Rasti's home.

This case was a difficult one and it needed all her concentration. She had visited Madjur twice before and had found her in difficulties both times. Madjur had fallen prey to rheumatoid arthritis at thirty-two, and now, at forty-one, she was semi-crippled by the disease.

The Asian woman opened the door slowly, and it was evident that she had been crying.

'I'm sorry, Sister Duncan,' Madjur said,

without any life in her voice, 'I'm feeling dreadful. I don't think I can face talking today.'

Frances hesitated, not pushing the visit. 'Are you in pain, Madjur?'

She nodded, leaning against the door. 'I can't move my knee and I feel sick.'

'May I take a quick look? Perhaps I can help?'

Reluctantly Madjur let her in, and Frances took her weight as they limped slowly into the front room. One knee in particular was swollen, tender to the touch and almost unbearable to move. The woman looked washed out, as though she didn't care whether she lived or died.

'I'm going to call the doctor,' Frances said, and, getting up from the settee on which there was a made-up bed, she phoned the surgery and asked Gill to ring the doctor on call for a visit.

About twenty minutes later Frances opened the door to Bruno. 'What's the trouble?' he asked quietly, towering over her as he walked into the narrow hallway.

Forgetting all her earlier antipathy, and just relieved to see help, she nodded towards the room. 'I think it's a particularly nasty flare-up. She's in a great deal of pain and the aspirin seem to be upsetting her. She's complaining of nausea and so she doesn't take them. A vicious circle, really, because now the pain is acute.'

He went through a thorough examination and finally decided to draw off some of the fluid around the knee with a needle and syringe. Frances bandaged it afterwards and together they made Madjur comfortable on the bed-settee. Bruno sat in the armchair next to it to talk to her, and Frances listened to his voice and felt comforted herself. He was gentle and sympathetic, and yet he made it clear to Madjur that she would have to consider the possibility of removing the bursa.

'No operations,' Madjur said heavily. 'My father had an operation and he never recovered.'

'He had the same complaint?' Bruno asked.

Madjur nodded. 'He was English and full of arthritis. My mother, who is from Delhi, has never had a day's illness in her life.'

Bruno nodded. 'I can understand your reticence, but we've had to draw off the fluid so often for you, I really think we must consider surgery. The bursa is being irritated by the injury to the nearby joint—the rheumatoid arthritis. The little pad becomes inflamed and filled with fluid. Not only that, but your hip is affected, and your ankle—'

'No!' Madjur's huge frightened eyes looked up from her gaunt face. 'Thank you, Dr Quillan . . . but no.' Her black hair was lifeless and thin, and Frances felt a pang of sadness for the beautiful young woman in a sari who gazed out from a wedding photo on the mantelpiece.

Madjur caught her gaze. 'You wouldn't recognise me, would you?'

Bruno said with a sigh, 'We could help, Madjur. I've mentioned the hip replacement before—I know you won't consider it, but at least go for the bursa. You won't have to wait in suspense for an eternity. I will arrange transport for you to a hospital where you can have the operation done under local anaesthetic, if you prefer. Twenty-four hours is all it will take.'

He received no response, however, and finally, after making her as comfortable as she could, Frances left, following Bruno to the cars. When they reached them he sighed frustratedly and shot his case into the front seat with a thump. 'We've been all through this before. She endures the corticosteroid drugs and the draining of fluid and grits her teeth. Even her neck is affected now. She's had generalised inflammation over the last two years—the hip is definitely worsening and she's developing ankylosis in that knee. I suppose suggesting we surgically take out the bursa—which is, after all, only the smallest piece of offending fibrous tissue—is like offering to paint the Eiffel with a paintbrush.'

Frances hesitated. 'I see from the careplan that she lives alone. Yet she's married, and has a fifteen-year-old daughter.'

'The marriage broke up. The husband went back to India with the daughter.'

'But they're all British subjects?'

Bruno nodded. 'It's a complicated set-up, but the long and the short of it is the in-laws wanted the child. The husband, I gather, couldn't cope with the disease and was finally persuaded to go back to Delhi. Madjur has been on her own for two years.'

'What about physiotherapy?'

'She refuses. She won't go near a hospital. She won't even ring me. I have the feeling sometimes that she just doesn't want to be here any more. I think she's lost the will to live.'

Frances sighed. 'Surely there's something else we can do to help? What about Social Services, or even some kind of counselling?'

He looked at her sharply. 'Don't you think I've tried? I can't physically force her into accepting help.'

Frances stiffened. 'No, of course not! I'm not a mind-reader, Dr Quillan! I would have been aware of what was going on if only you'd discussed Madjur's case with me beforehand, so I was fully in the picture. I'm sorry to sound like a record stuck in a groove, but that's a fact!' She stonily tucked the careplan into her bag. 'Well, I mustn't delay you any longer.'

He jerked open the door of the Range Rover; and she thought that he was going to jump in and leave her standing on the pavement, but instead he turned back to her with dark brows raised. 'Have you thought over what we were talking about?'

She looked up at him and her heart tightened. 'What do you mean?'

'Look,' he grunted, and turned back towards her. 'I'm asking for Jack's sake as well. You know, you made quite an impression on him. He made me promise to ask you over . . . will you come?'

She couldn't believe this! 'B-but that's blackmail!'

Suddenly he laughed and shook his head. 'Now, why am I not surprised to hear you say something like that?' He jumped up into the Range Rover seat and slammed the door. 'Sevenish?' he shouted over the roar of the engine. 'And don't eat!'

*   *   *

Frances sniffed the barbecue even before she rang the bell—a delicious odour that mingled with the honeysuckle and the mown grass in a summery haze over the gardens. Not that it did anything to dispel her disbelief at finding herself obedient to Bruno Quillan's command. It annoyed her beyond reason that he'd levelled the boy against her conscience. He must have known that was the only reason she would turn up on this particular doorstep again!

Jack opened the door, dressed in a sweatshirt and jeans. 'Hello, Fran. We've got a

53

barbecue. Grandma said careful of the midges. Dad's shaving because he's only just come in. Do you want to see my computer?'

With this barrage of information, Frances was tugged instantly upstairs and introduced to the sanctum of sanctums—Jack's computer room. After initiating her, he grabbed her hand and pulled her back along the landing past the bathroom. 'Dad's in there, but he can't hear you 'cos he's shaving with an electrical razor,' he told her—which wasn't difficult to guess because of the familiar drift of tangy lemon and a high-pitched buzzing 'Now come and see the pool.'

'The pool?' She raised her eyebrows.

Jack nodded excitedly. 'It's not open yet, because of the leaves and stuff blowing in, but Dad's going to get it ready soon.'

En route downstairs, Jack waved to a glass door leading off the hall. 'Grandma lives through there in the granny annexe.' Then he hauled her through a leafy green conservatory to a veranda at the back.

In the garden, a large green canvas was battened down to the grass. 'The pool,' Jack announced, and lifted a flap for her to look under.

She peered under. 'Is there water in there?' He giggled. 'Only rainwater. But Dad's going to fill it soon.'

'Can you swim?'

Jack lifted his shoulders. 'Of course. I have

to for my asthma.'

Frances looked duly admonished. 'It looks fun.'

'It is. There's Grandma.' He pointed to a woman in wellies, dungarees and a battered straw hat. She was turning sausages on a spit and waved to them.

'Over here, Frances,' she called.

Jack whispered conspiratorially, 'I'll fetch Dad.'

She grabbed his shoulder. 'No—don't! I mean . . . I shan't stop long, Jack. Don't trouble your father.' But he hadn't heard, or deliberately pretended not to, and went tearing off. Frances gritted her teeth. Nothing else for it, she realised, but to make her way over.

Wishing she had worn jeans instead of the long, summery skirt which swirled around her legs, she found herself wondering what Bruno had told his family about her coming tonight. But all concerns evaporated as she approached and Jack's grandmother held out her hand.

'Hello, Frances. Jack hasn't stopped talking about you.' She smiled. 'And Bruno hasn't said a word—which means you've made an impact on both.'

Frances heard herself laughing, conscious of how much she liked Rosa. They chatted for a few moments and then Bruno appeared, dressed in cream slacks and a shirt with so many colours it was virtually blinding, and which, for a moment, took her mind off the feeling of sheer panic.

Rosa giggled. 'All you need now are shades, Bruno!'

He smiled wryly and patted the pocket of the shirt, bringing out a pair which he slipped on. They were the sort that reflected everything, including the red-hot heat of the barbecue. As laughter peeled up into the evening, air he reached over Frances's head and took Rosa's straw hat, thrusting it in carefree fashion on his dark head.

For someone who, it seemed, had an entirely different persona away from his work environment, she saw that he had a capacity to take himself lightly. And—dared she admit it?—she was flattered at the way in which he looked at her—even through those dreadful shades!

CHAPTER THREE

The evening went on until a slow moon moved over them and darkened the trees to tall silhouettes, and only the firelight, around which they sat, lit up their faces as they talked.

Eventually Rosa stretched and looked at Jack, who was muffled by a sweater and absorbed in swatting the fireflies trespassing near the remains of the food. 'Past my bedtime and yours,' she said tiredly, blinking. 'Come on, young man, help me in with some of the debris.' She stood up, and as Jack meandered off to the kitchen she bent down and touched Frances's arm. 'I can't thank you enough, my dear, for helping us with Jack. You really are a treasure.'

Frances forced herself not to look at Bruno. 'It was no trouble, Rosa.'

'And you will come to see us again?'

She hesitated. 'Well . . . I'm only in Cerne Carey for six months—'

'All summer?' Rosa interrupted, and smiled. 'How wonderful. Jack will be so pleased. Now, goodnight you two—and don't let the midges devour you!'

She walked away and Frances swallowed. Why hadn't she simply said no, she wasn't expecting to call again? No. Easy enough. Two small letters pinned together to make a negative. Instead she felt railroaded, and she was sure that it wasn't Rosa's fault. But she did know whose fault it was!

'Why didn't you tell her?' she demanded, and jerked her head around to the man who sat in a deckchair, terrible shirt open against a hard brown chest. She'd taken a breath as she'd fallen against it earlier when playing rounders, her fall exposing a multitude of smooth brown hairs which clambered over the hard muscle beneath as the shirt had ripped open.

She'd tried to ignore him as he'd helped her to her feet, but ignoring a man like Bruno Quillan was virtually impossible. Physically, he was rampantly athletic and vitally male, and his presence had felt blatantly sensual against her. Not that he'd held on to her any longer than necessary. He hadn't needed to. She had been aware of every moment of his body, so long and supple, a combination of animal strength and human energy that seemed mind-blowing—as if he released all his stress and tension in the channel of aggressive, hard worked movement.

'Tell Rosa what?' he asked with a frown.

'That I only came tonight as an exception.'

He shrugged. 'Because she wanted to show her appreciation and because it would have hurt her to tell her you won't see Jack any more.'

She glared at him. 'You planned this, didn't you?'

He leant forward, the hard, bronzed muscle of forearms perched on knees, dark eyes raised up to her blue ones. 'I hoped you would come. Yes.'

'You've put me in an impossible position.' She sighed angrily. 'I don't want to be rude to Rosa and I don't want to hurt Jack either.' She suddenly remembered the pleasure of the boy's smile—a small, secret smile he'd given her on occasions throughout the evening, as though they knew something the world didn't know—and her heart clenched at the thought of it.

Too late she was aware of the dangers. Too late she had become fond of the child, and was fully aware of the attachment which might follow.

'What can come of it?' she demanded, keeping her voice low. 'I'm just someone passing through his life. I don't want to befriend him one day and desert him the next.'

He shrugged dismissively. 'I couldn't agree more—but why make such a high drama out of it? All he needs at the moment is friendship. He's suddenly met someone who has given him some very real support during a rough patch. Can't you accept that for what it is?'

She stared into the fire. 'You make it sound easy, but it isn't.'

He nodded. 'Fair enough. I'm not suggesting you make a habit out of seeing him, but just pop in occasionally when you've time, that's all.'

She took a breath. 'Occasionally?'

'That's not too much to ask, is it?' He opened his hands. 'And I promise I shan't get in the way.'

She stood up, her body framed by the embers of the fire. 'I'll think about it. It's late. I must go.'

'It's barely half past nine,' he told her with a quickly flicked glance at the heavy band of gold on his wrist.

'Which is late enough for me. Please thank Rosa . . . I appreciate her hospitality.'

She moved away from the fire, thinking that she must have been mad even to enter into a conversation about Jack, fast becoming her Achilles' heel. She had come here expecting an apology for what had happened in the garden that night—an excuse, even, for not having contacted her during a whole week in which she had agonised over actually allowing him to kiss her. The man certainly had audacity!

He grabbed her wrist and she spun back, feeling the contraction of her muscles in response—though not in her arms, but way down deep in the centre of her being, in a place she had hardly known existed until now.

'I wanted to explain tonight,' he told her as he forced her to face him, his hands hard about her wrists, 'about why I didn't contact you last week. I had time off because of Jack . . . and I thought you would guess what had happened.'

It was a pathetic excuse and he knew it. He just didn't know how to get out of a situation he'd landed himself in and he thought that by avoiding the issue it would disappear! She glared at him 'You expect me to believe you didn't come to work because—'

'Because Jack had a severe asthma attack in the night and was wretched in the morning,' he repeated patiently, but she decided that she'd heard enough. Why couldn't he just come out

60

with it and say he'd made a dreadful mistake in kissing her and was using Jack as an excuse?

She wriggled her wrists free, and in the light of the dying embers tipped up her chin 'Goodnight, Dr Quillan.'

His eyes were glimmering as he stared at her. 'And what about Jack?'

'You know how I feel about Jack!'

'I hope I do. I hope you won't let our . . . differences . . . affect your relationship with him.'

It wasn't fair! It just wasn't fair. He was just piling on the guilt, and whichever way she turned she felt trapped. But words could no longer express her feelings, and she turned and walked to the veranda and into the house. She passed Rosa's door, and at the bottom of the stairs hesitated as she looked up to Jack's room. Then she opened the front door and closed it quietly, and hurried to the Clio.

Inside, she let out a long breath. Then her eyes caught the sweater on the seat beside her. She'd forgotten it again. But nothing was going to drag her back into that house. Not tonight or ever.

*   *   *

The week strained, on. She called on Sarah Clark and noticed that Freddie was crying and irritable again. Sarah herself was distant, and insisted that there was nothing wrong. So what could she do other than make a note to visit the next week?

Bruno had called at Gabriel Bally's and left a note in the book for Frances to do a follow-up check.

Gabriel Bally's current assessment in his careplan was written up as epigastric discomfort, dyspnoea and palpitation. Bruno had also recorded a cough and pain and nausea. The oesophagoscopy had confirmed a hiatus hernia, and he'd advised trying to reduce the problem before considering surgery.

The patient sat anxiously in his reclining chair in his lovely home, and his wife a surprisingly young woman, perhaps half her husband's age with striking silver-blonde hair—watched rather restlessly as Frances studied the assessment and asked how he was feeling.

'He's ill,' his wife broke in impatiently, 'can't you see that? He can't work. This has gone on for too long!'

Frances studied Gabriel Bally. He was highly coloured and sweating and he did look thinner—or perhaps the anxiety in his face had merely deepened over the weeks. Carefully she said, 'Dr Quillan has asked me to go over a few helpful tips—like eating small, bland meals, and supper, for instance, is best taken three to four hours before retiring—'

'We do that already.' The young wife sighed

impatiently. 'We never eat out any more—at least, not together. We never go anywhere or do anything.'

Up till now, Frances realised, she hadn't had a response from her patient. He was truly a man who had become introvert—though perhaps before his illness he had been a quiet man anyway.

'And you take your antacid and laxative, Mr Bally?' she prodded gently.

'Yes, yes.' Her patient's voice was weary. 'After meals and before going to bed. I do everything I'm told to do—'

'But none of it makes any difference,' Mrs. Bally cut in icily. 'He's up roaming around half the night with indigestion.'

Frances saw the visible flinch in the man's troubled eyes. She waited for him to respond, but he just dropped his head and studied his hands.

'How about your bed?' Frances glanced down at her notes to see if anyone had advised raising it. When she looked up, the couple were staring at her as if she'd asked them where they kept the family silver.

She said quickly, 'The head of your bed should be raised about twenty-three centimetres, to help prevent reflux into the oesophagus—'

Suddenly, and quite without warning, the woman jumped to her feet and, eyes filling with tears, she ran from the room, slamming the door behind her with such velocity that Frances actually saw one of the oil paintings on the wall judder.

Gabriel Bally looked stricken, attempted to get up, and then, rubbing a hand over his face, sank back in the chair again.

Frances gazed in bewilderment at the door. 'Did I say something to offend Mrs Bally?'

He shook his head slowly. 'It's not your fault. You simply touched a raw nerve. My wife is very young, just twenty-five, and she finds it hard to cope with my illness. I was quite fit when we married two years ago.'

My age, Frances thought in surprise, unable to understand why, even if Mrs Bally was sensitive to sickness, such a severe reaction should evolve from simple advice about a bed.

Gabriel Bally soon provided the answer. 'You won't find this in there,' he said, gesturing to the careplan, 'but I suppose I'll have to say—we . . . consulted Dr Quillan on a private matter.' He shrugged tiredly, shaking his head. 'We're trying for a child and it hasn't been successful. Naturally, Petra is convinced it's because I'm impotent.'

His face crumpled into a mask of unhappiness. 'I'm afraid—well, I'm just not as adventurous as I was. It's very tiresome for Petra, who is a healthy, active young woman. I can't go to the gym and exercise. I can't even go for a long walk any more. I disturb her sleep—lying on any number of pillows to ease the discomfort—and some positions in bed, if you understand, really are intolerable. Mentioning the bed just seemed to be the last nail in the coffin of our sex-life, I'm afraid.'

Frances sighed. What could she say? Why hadn't Bruno Quillan alerted her to the problem, or at least, if he didn't want to betray confidences, warned her that the situation between the Ballys was highly sensitive? For the same reason, she supposed angrily, that he hadn't briefed her on other cases in that first week, when it had been so vital to discover the true facts relating to people's illnesses. OK, he was a busy man, and he might not have had time, but somehow, some way, he should have made time to discuss with her inherent problems such as this.

Gabriel Bally looked up and shrugged. 'Let's leave it at that for today, shall we? Let me see you out.'

She felt dreadful, but she realised that there was nothing she could do. He obviously wanted to speak to his wife, and making an apology would only mean further embarrassment all round.

He eased himself from the chair and Frances saw that he was a tall man and probably, when in good health and without the worrying high colour, quite attractive. But now he looked much older than forty-nine, and was almost like an old man in his movements. Marrying a much younger woman was obviously having its drawbacks.

She left and made her way back to the practice. She felt angry and upset, for she had been made to look a fool and, what was worse, an interfering fool. But as she neared the surgery she calmed down, patently aware that it was always the doctor's decision that counted. If Bruno had decided not to take her into his confidence about the Ballys then that was it. She had to accept it. And as he hadn't mentioned the problem obviously he had wanted to keep her ignorant of it. If she hadn't mentioned the bed today . . . oh, well, one down to experience, Frances thought with a sigh, and decided to put it firmly out of mind. Although at the moment she felt like it, a head-on with Bruno Quillan she could definitely do without.

Not expecting to catch Bruno before he left on his calls, she walked in. The teatime rush had quietened down. She chatted with Nigel and Tristan, making notes as she went. She was becoming used to each doctor's patients and was able now to talk about them with a degree of confidence. Oddly enough, the patients who concerned her most were Bruno's. But Freddie Clark was to all intents and purposes a thriving baby, and Gabriel Bally had had a barium meal, chest X-rays and an exploratory op and they could find nothing except the hernia . . .

'Penny for them?' a deep, voice asked as she studied the monitor of the computer.

66

She swirled around. 'Bru . . . I mean, Dr Quillan.' Her face flushed as she caught Gill's stare across Reception.

He tilted his head. 'Have you a moment?' She felt herself tense. 'Now?'

He raised firm eyebrows. 'Now.'

'I—I've rather a lot—'

'It'll only take a few moments.'

She suppressed her reluctance and nodded. 'If you insist. I'll just finish this and I'll be in.'

She returned her gaze to the computer, seeing nothing but a red mist, and tapped at the keys ferociously.

'What's going on, you dark horse?' a female voice whispered in her ear, and she jumped and blinked up at Gill.

'Nothing! Why?'

'Tell that to the marines,' Gill laughed, then squeezed her arm. 'Good luck to you, I say. Just don't get yourself hurt . . . He's a cool customer, is our Dr Quillan. He's married to his work and has a perfect set-up at home. Many women have tried—and many have failed.'

Frances looked up in surprise. 'What on earth do you mean?'

Gill nodded. 'Like young Suzie Collins over there—and even Meg Fellows.'

Frances stared across the room at the young part-time receptionist working at the desk. She was dark and slender, and Frances had often noticed her unusual slanting eyes, thinking how beautiful they were. She knew that Suzie was single now but that she'd had a boyfriend with whom she had lived. She'd never linked Bruno with her—nor, indeed, the vivacious Meg.

'Surprised?' Gill laughed quietly. 'Thought I'd just mention it. Better you know how the land lies. Especially since . . .'

Frances waited. 'Especially since . . .?'

Gill looked embarrassed. 'Look, perhaps it's not up to me to say, but the physical similarity between you and Lindsay Quillan is astonishing. Didn't you know?'

Frances swallowed. 'No, as a matter of fact, I didn't.'

'Oh, lor', trust me to put my foot in it!'

'It's all right, Gill. Better I know.' She hesitated. 'Not that it matters, of course.'

The receptionist agreed, but her expression was rueful.

Five minutes later, in Bruno's room, Frances was staring at him, her mind blitzed from the news that Gill had just relayed—though she realised that she had sunk low enough to listen to the gossip without much protest. Still, it was only human nature to wonder how deeply he had been involved with Suzie or Meg Fellows, but more shocking, she found, was Gill's remark on her similarity to Lindsay.

'Horns or tail?' he asked as she hovered by his desk.

'Sorry?'

'Well, either I've sprouted horns or grown a tail. And without a mirror I can't tell.'

She shook her head quickly. 'Oh, I was just thinking about something Gill said.'

He frowned at her. 'What a disappointment.'

She looked up at him. 'Why?'

'Because I was hoping you were thinking about what you might do at the weekend.'

She took a breath. 'If prying into my private life is what you asked me in here, for, then—'

'No, I wasn't attempting to pry,' he interrupted gently. 'All I was going to say was that the pool will be set up by then. Jack said you'd expressed an interest in seeing it.'

'I'm sure Jack has plenty of friends he can ask over,' she deflected quickly.

'Think about it.'

'I have—thank you—and it's still no.'

He sat and watched her, hands folded on the desk.

'Is that all you wanted to see me about?' she demanded uncomfortably.

'Isn't it enough?'

She gave him a withering glare and turned, thinking that she would like to push him right back over the chair and off his high perch when he called out, 'Bring your bikini and your water wings.'

*   *   *

69

It turned out to be the warmest May for years. Frances had kept to her no, then had been rung by Rosa and invited for lunch on Saturday. And then Jack had come on the phone and asked her. She hated her capitulation, but the one saving grace was that she knew Bruno wouldn't be there. She had seen the rota sheet pinned up on the office board and she knew that he was on call.

She took with her an armful of sweet-smelling summer flowers under cellophane, a bottle of wine, some apple juice for Jack and, because she couldn't think of anything else, a frozen Black Forest gateau. Hesitating over the sweater, which still lay on a chair in her bedroom, she snatched it up and flung it in the boot of the Clio, as though by hiding it from sight she would effectively erase Bruno from her day.

Jack was in the pool already when she arrived, swimming breaststroke. Her eyes nearly popped out of her head when she saw another figure beside him, glisteningly naked except for a brief pair of black trunks which clung to the masculine firmness of the hard, wet hips.

She could neither turn back nor go on. It was Rosa who jolted her into movement as she came up behind her.

'Change in Bruno's room, Frances,' she said sweetly. 'I've put fresh towels and sunscreen there for you . . .'

'Oh . . . yes, right . . . Er, I thought Bruno was on call?'

Rosa nodded. 'He is. So don't be surprised to see him take a flying leap from the pool any moment.'

With a measure of relief, Frances dived away. What she had seen had given her goose bumps and made a flood of heat envelop her. Bruno had tremendous shape—and she was sure that he knew it. Did he work out, she wondered, to achieve those muscular broad shoulders and slim hips? The blade-flat abdomen had shimmered tantalisingly in the sunshine, and beneath, those firm thighs had cut the water with force.

Help! she thought as she wandered up the stairs. What am I thinking about? How was she going to concentrate? Greg was a good-looking guy, obsessed with keeping fit, but somehow Bruno looked different, less synthetically honed, more naturally well built. All those dark hairs washed over tawny skin. Even from a distance she'd noticed them. Like a huge, wet brown bear emerging from a lake.

She stopped on the stairs, took a breath and told herself, You are an idiot, Frances Duncan. Why let the man have such an effect on you? Greg hadn't made her feel this way, inflicted such damage on her nervous system, and she had known Greg for two years.

She found the bedroom, gingerly opening

71

the door. It had to be Bruno's because of the lemony-lime fragrance that always clung to him. A light, large room with blinds, not curtains. Thick chocolate carpet. A huge double bed with a luxuriously patterned throw. Had he slept here with Lindsay?

She gazed about the room, looking for photographs. She was curious to see her likeness, but she was disappointed. Dragging back her mind, she saw towels draped over a rosewood dresser, and she began to peel off her shorts and sweatshirt and dig in her haversack for her swimsuit.

She'd decided against the bikini, thank heavens! The swimsuit was revealing enough—high legs and a looped neckline made the white one-piece quite daring—but it was at least all in one. She stared in the long wall mirror.

'Frances Duncan,' she said with a sigh as she curled her hair up into a thick golden topknot, 'ignore him. Let him know he doesn't make one iota of difference to your equilibrium.'

Which was exactly what she intended to do as she padded down the stairs in flip-flops, a towel in her arms. Rosa had music going in the kitchen and the house was filled with summery scents and a salady smell which emanated thickly from the kitchen.

She pulled herself up straight and, heart in mouth, quickened her step to the veranda. Bruno ambled towards her, shedding water on the grass as he went. His eyes went from top to toe, taking in every inch.

'Here, let me take your towel,' he said, with open admiration in his eyes, and reached out.

But she clung to it like a limpet. Then, catching his amusement, dropped it like a hot brick. His eyes ran greedily over her again. For a moment she felt rooted to the spot, as though he were looking right through her into her secret thoughts.

'Ready?' he asked throatily.

For what? she wondered. But she didn't have to wonder long, as he scooped her up bodily in his arms, tossing away the towel, and, as she screamed, ran full tilt with her to the pool and jumped in.

The water was freezing at first. She gasped underneath it, feeling the cold bottom on the soles of her feet as everything turned into blurry slow motion. She was aware that she was still entangled in his arms, her hair spinning in the water like fawn seaweed. She forced open her eyes just in time to feel him drag her close, and she was encompassed in hard muscle and moving, living, incredible strength. She felt the water throb in her ears— throb, throb, throb—or was it her heart?

Then suddenly they were flying to the surface, and they broke it together, the fresh, clean air filling her lungs as she gasped and gasped again.

'Warm enough for you?' he shouted,

throwing back his dark head and laughing

'It's f-freezing!' she gasped, bobbing around like a top, thrusting her hair from her eyes.

Neither of them saw Jack dive in and swim under their legs to pop up beside Frances with a loud 'Yeehah!'

'Oh, Jack!' She trod water and struggled to the side, aware that both males were having the time of their lives at her expense.

She got her breath back and glared at them from between the long wet strands of her hair. 'OK,' she called with a malevolent grin, now that she could breathe again and was used to the water, 'you'll both pay for that!'

She just heard Jack's scream of delight as she turned upside down in the water and dived to the bottom. Above her she could see four legs thrashing and the water churning around them in their effort to get away from her. But she was a strong, fast swimmer, thanks to two hefty brothers who had always expected her to keep up with them.

A second later she had Jack in her sights, and before he could yank himself out of the pool she had his waist and gently pushed him up, turned him around in the water and dunked him again. It was only mild horseplay—she didn't want to cause him too much excitement—and as she broke the surface beside him she saw laughter erupt as he threw himself away from her and made for the other end of the pool.

She hadn't bargained for Bruno, though, who swam up beside her and dragged her down. This time she spun in his arms and slithered away like a fish, meeting the surface with a careful inward breath and swimming fast down the length of the pool back to Jack.

They all ended up in heaps of breathless laughter on the steps.

Bruno lounged back, breathing hard, his body glistening wetly in the sunshine, brown and relaxed so the muscle looked as if it were covered with silk. 'You're some swimmer,' he chuckled, and Jack nodded his wet head in agreement.

'I had two brothers to keep up with,' she giggled, and relaxed her long legs on the steps. 'If I couldn't keep up with them, they wouldn't take me swimming with them.'

Jack slithered down beside her, suddenly interested. 'What do they do now?'

'They're both soldiers in the Army,' she told him, getting her breath back. 'One's in Germany and the other in Singapore.'

He nodded slowly, chewing on his lip. 'What about your mum and dad?'

'Dad's a Royal Engineer and my mum . . . is just a mum—though she was once a nurse in the QAs.' Jack frowned at the abbreviation and she added quickly, 'Short for Queen Alexandra's Royal Army Nursing Corps. That's where I did my training too.'

'Did you live in Germany or Sing . . .

Singapore?'

Frances shook her head. 'I went to boarding-school whilst they travelled to different postings. I used to fly out to visit them on holidays, though, with the other girls from service families.'

Suddenly an air of tension settled around them, and Bruno stared at her whilst Jack hesitated, a big frown on his small forehead; she could tell that he wanted to ask her something. But Bruno tapped him on the shoulder and said softly, 'Run in and ask Grandma if she wants us for lunch, will you, Jack?'

The boy got up slowly and, dragging a towel around him from the poolside, loped off to the house.

Bruno rested large wet forearms on his knees and looked up at her. 'I wasn't aware you went to boarding-school.'

She shrugged, shivering, and he reached across and threaded a towel around her shoulders. 'Dad could hardly tow us around the world with him,' she answered shortly, stiffening against the touch of his fingers. 'They went to Germany, Naples, Kowloon— just about everywhere.' She swallowed hard. 'It was a way of life you didn't argue with.'

He nodded slowly, drawing a wet strand of hair gently from her, face and out from the towel, arranging it behind her ear, and her body convulsed as she felt the touch of his

76

fingers again as they drifted over her neck. 'Did you miss them?'

She hesitated for a moment, unsteadied by her reaction and by the question. Pulling herself together, she shrugged, remembering the battles she'd had to fight at the all-girls school in order to establish herself, and the initial feeling of loneliness and isolation. 'Oh, I missed them.' She sighed reflectively. 'But there wasn't an alternative—not with the army. Dad was ambitious and Mum went wherever he did. We got used to being away from them—but then, I was quite a tough little character.'

He looked wry. 'So it seems.' His eyes were soft as he studied her flawless skin, the dove-blue eyes with their exotic flecks of grey, which shone out brilliantly against the white of her swimsuit; and the sun-bleached tawnyness of her wet limbs. She felt herself blushing as they sat in silence for a moment, the sun playing down on their wet skin. Then with a sigh he said softly, 'I'm sending Jack to boarding-school in September. Did you know?'

So Richard Grove had been right! Frances sat up, her jaw falling open.

Bruno stared down at the wet steps between his long brown legs. 'It hasn't been an easy decision,' he said grimly, 'but it seems the only sensible one—the only alternative for a boy like Jack. An only child—too sensitive for his own good. A child who has few friends and prefers to play with a computer rather than other boys.'

She felt her heart quicken and forced herself to remain silent, but he lifted his head and sought her eyes. She tried to avoid them, staring back at the safety of the blue water. Jack wasn't her concern.

But Bruno had caught the expression on her face.

She lifted her chin and looked at him. 'I can't believe he's unhappy at home.'

He shrugged. 'No, not in a physical sense. But emotionally . . .? I can't make up for Lindsay.'

'I don't think he expects you to.'

He frowned. 'What makes you say that?'

Knowing that she was doing exactly what she had promised herself not to do—becoming involved—she hesitated. 'Jack understands more than you think he does. He's very mature for his age.'

'And?'

'Are you asking for my opinion?'

He paused, and then nodded. 'You're obviously qualified . . . yes, yes I am.'

She took a breath and stared at the deep, intensely brown eyes so coolly regarding her. 'If Jack were my child,' she said slowly, running her tongue tentatively over her lips, 'I wouldn't consider boarding-school as an alternative. I would look closer to home. But then, he isn't my son—he's yours.'

Bruno stared at her for a long while, his dark gaze running over her face, studying her fine, classical features and soft damp skin haloed by a veil of long wet hair dripping over her shoulders and down her back.

Eventually he stood up and held out a hand. Reluctantly she allowed herself to be lifted, her body shuddering under the clinging white cloth, her small hand held firmly in his grasp.

'A pity,' he said, and she didn't know what he was referring to—other than her disagreement with him over boarding-school.

Before she could move he picked up another, drier towel and gently pressed it around her shoulders, his touch making her shiver as he began to push it slowly, across her wet skin—under the curve of her chin and slowly and tenderly down the slope of her neck.

She almost stopped breathing.

A cascade of goose bumps erupted over her bare shoulders. She stared at him and he at her. The May breeze whispered over the proud little mountains of flesh he had caused.

She shivered and swallowed.

'A pity,' he said again, his voice deeper now. 'You're built for motherhood, do you know that?'

The remark left her breathless. 'I beg your p-pardon?'

He lifted her wet hair and his fingers brushed the nape of her neck. 'A compliment,

my sweet Frances. You're a natural—
biologically . . .' he stared down at her
feminine figure, his eyes praising every inch of
her '. . . and emotionally.'

She gulped, aware that her throat was as
dry as a bone. 'And . . . wh-what makes you say
that?'

He dropped the towel and stared hungrily at
her lips. 'Just about everything,' he whispered
huskily. Then, reaching out, his fingers had
almost encircled her waist before Jack came
bounding out onto the veranda to tell them
that lunch was ready.

CHAPTER FOUR

The call came after lunch as they were
organising the ping-pong table in the
conservatory. Frances was trying to think up
an excuse to leave, the intimacy of his remarks
whispered by the pool still making her tremble
when she allowed herself to think about them.
If Jack hadn't come along, what would have
been her reply?

'It'll be a call-out, I expect,' Rosa said with a
shrug as Bruno hurried away to answer it.

Jack bounced a ball moodily. 'It always is.'

Rosa began to screw the nets to the table.
'Well, perhaps Frances would like a game,' she
suggested cheerfully.

80

Feeling that she could hardly decline, she nodded. 'OK, perhaps just a quick one. But you'll probably thrash me.'

Bruno lunged back in, thrusting the proverbial hand through his hair. 'I have to leave, I'm afraid. But I shouldn't be too long.'

Rosa smiled. 'Oh, well, at least we managed lunch. Come on, then, Jack, let's finish setting up the table.'

'Sorry,' Bruno sighed, raising apologetic shoulders.

Frances found herself watching him as he whizzed around collecting his things. He'd changed into navy blue trousers, sweatshirt and trainers after lunch, and his deep brown hair was for once brushed back into order after the swim.

'Shouldn't be too long,' he said with a regretful smile as he made for the front door. 'Will you be here when I come back?'

She stood stiffly in the hall with an armful of small bats. 'I doubt it. Is it something serious?'

'Gabriel Bally. Chest pain.'

Frances caught her breath. 'Oh, I wonder—'

'Talk to you later—wait for me if you can. We can swim later in the day, before the sun goes down.' Then he shot out to the Range Rover and she saw the vehicle pull out in a cloud of dust.

Well, if he thought she was going to spend her afternoon waiting for a repeat performance of the morning, he was out of luck. She had no desire to swim again and, despite her secret pleasure at being with Jack and Rosa, she would be gone by the time he returned.

The thought of Gabriel Bally irked her. He'd been under some increasing pressure lately and she hadn't liked the look of his colour. Hopefully it wasn't a cardiovascular problem, but the signs had been there when she'd seen him—although she hadn't really registered them consciously. Had trouble sparked between the couple after her visit? If only she had been more in the picture when she'd talked to them. But what was done was done, and it couldn't be changed now.

She went back to the conservatory and played several games with Jack, and was truly thrashed until on the third game he began to pale and his asthma started.

Rosa handled it calmly enough and Jack took his medication; sitting down in front of the TV to stare at the screen. He seemed preoccupied, and Frances decided that now was the time to leave.

'Must you go?' Rosa asked disappointedly.

Just then the phone rang and she answered it, turning to Frances to whisper, 'Bruno. He's been held up.'

'Did he say how his patient was?' Frances asked, but Rosa shook her head, and as they lapsed into silence she saw that Jack had fallen asleep on the settee. She trod slowly over to check his breathing. 'Seems to have settled,' she murmured, and Rosa nodded.

Minutes later she retrieved her things from Bruno's room. The usual accoutrements of men overflowed on the dresser and a few shirts hung limply on the back of a silk-covered chaise longue—not at all a man's piece of furniture. Had it belonged to Lindsay? she wondered. Frances blinked. She was becoming perversely obsessed with thinking about her—more so now that she knew they were so much alike.

'I wish you would have supper with us,' Rosa said downstairs, wiping her hands on a pinny. Already she had begun to prepare supper in the kitchen.

Frances laughed softly. 'I've a home to go to—albeit a very small one.'

Rosa chuckled. 'Just as long as you aren't leaving because you feel you must without Bruno here.'

'On the contrary . . .' And then she paused, tempted for a moment to accept. If she stayed, perhaps she would discover more from Rosa about Lindsay. Then sensibly she resisted the temptation and shook her head. 'It's been a super day, but I think I'm about ready to crash out. Saturdays aren't usually half so energetic.'

Rosa laughed again. 'Not for us either. Bruno is rarely here on a Saturday.'

'Because of the practice?'

Rosa nodded as she walked with her to the

door. 'With the change-over to fund-holding he doesn't have much time left for luxuries. Emergency surgery in the mornings usually leads on to a call or two, and then if one or the other doctors wants time off—well, you'll know the routine, of course, being a nurse.' She paused on the doorstep. 'Have you heard about Jack in September?'

'Boarding-school?' Frances bit her lip and nodded. 'How does Jack feel about it?'

The older woman sighed. 'He's trying to handle it, bless him. Bruno knows what's best, I suppose. The trouble is, he's such a sensitive little soul.'

*   *   *

A remark Frances mulled over for the rest of the weekend. She had palpably felt Rosa's apprehension, which obviously reflected Jack's. Surely there was another alternative to boarding-school? Knowing Bruno, though, she supposed that no one was going to get him to change his mind

On Monday, she went into the surgery to find that he had written in the DN's book: 'Frances, please see me'.

She asked Gill if she knew what it was about and whether it could wait until after lunch, but Gill seemed vague, and as Frances stood undecidedly in the middle of a chaotic Reception Bruno walked along the corridor

84

and beckoned her to his room. 'Hold my list up for a moment or two, will you, Suzie?' he called, and the young woman looked up—and, Frances noticed, blushed as she stared at him.

'It's the Ballys,' Bruno said shortly as, in his consulting room, he shut the door behind them. 'When I arrived there on Saturday Gabriel was experiencing bouts of chest pain. They'd obviously had one almighty row, making his condition a great deal worse.'

Trying to ignore the fact that he'd not even said good morning to her, she frowned. 'The hernia?'

'Not this time. I examined him and took a blood specimen to identify thyroid or anaemia, or any other possible cause of the pain, but I'm certain it was angina.'

'Angina?' She hesitated. Then she nodded slowly. 'I don't think I'm surprised.'

Bruno looked up from the desk sharply. 'What makes you say that?'

'His general condition and the worry he's had . . .'

'Which is what I want to talk to you about. Petra Bally has made an official complaint— to me—that you were aware of their marital difficulties and that you must have come upon those private details somewhere—if I didn't disclose them.'

Frances sank into the patient's seat and stared at him incredulously. 'But that's ridiculous! It was just a coincidence—'

85

'Something was said, then?'

Frances felt the hairs on the back of her neck rise. 'Not intentionally—'

'Intentionally or not, she feels I've betrayed their confidence.'

Frances shook her head. 'All that happened—'

He stood up. 'Frances, I haven't time for this, I'm afraid. I just thought you should know. I've sent Gabriel in for tests—chest X-ray, ECG and lipids and a possible radioisotope scan. And don't call around there this week or you may just find yourself confronting a very angry young woman.'

Frances realised that she was being dismissed—but if Petra Bally was angry, it was nothing to what she felt at this moment. And he wasn't even listening to her side of the story!

'Ask Suzie to send my next one in, would you?' Already his head was bent to the computer.

She counted to ten and waited. Not so much as a by-your-leave! She gave him one last glare, which he was quite oblivious to, and left the room. Before walking through to Reception, she tried to rationalise it all.

It was purely spite on Petra Bally's part, and that hurt—for she had done nothing to incur it. But it didn't hurt half as much as Bruno's attitude. He believed the woman; that was clear.

She walked into the waiting room and up to the desk and told Suzie Collins that the next patient could go in. The receptionist nodded but said nothing, and without any hesitation opened the gate dividing them, walked past her and disappeared down the hall and into Bruno's room. Frances just caught the drift of his voice as the door closed, and his tone seemed soft.

She couldn't believe how distressed she felt. He had time for Suzie, but he hadn't given her a second in which to explain herself over the Ballys.

'You're getting paranoid,' Frances muttered as she left and walked to the car. A condition she felt was intensifying as she called to see her next patient, little Freddie Clark.

Sarah Clark was pale and subdued when she arrived. Freddie was in his cot crying, and when Frances picked him up he was hot and, she suspected, distressed. But she didn't want to alienate Sarah, who said very little as she stood at the back of the nursery.

Frances curled the baby into her shoulder and he took a breath, his tiny little body juddering. She asked how the breast-feeding was going.

'He hasn't much of an appetite lately,' Sarah responded tonelessly.

Frances studied the pale, drawn face, her sense of unease deepening. 'And what about the sickness?'

The baby's mother shrugged. 'He's finicky. Not like my little girl. She was always hungry and ate well.'

'Do you mean he has no interest in his feeds, or that he regurgitates it afterwards?'

Frances could see that the young mum was confused. She didn't want to sound as though she were cross-questioning, but the child on her shoulder did not feel the solid little baby he should be by now.

Then, quite suddenly, Freddie vomited. The violent stomach contraction reverberated against her shoulder and, to her dismay, the vomit which she wiped from her uniform was offensive both in texture and smell.

'He's dirtied your dress,' Sarah remarked distantly, almost as though she were in a daydream.

Frances laid Freddie back in his cot. 'Is this vomiting becoming usual after each feed?'

The answer was, as she suspected, in the affirmative. Bearing in mind Sarah's seemingly confused state, Frances bent over and began to remove his babygro, explaining that she was just going to check him over before she left. Something told her that the search would reveal a clue, and sure enough Freddie began to cry, screwing up his little red face and clenching his tiny fists. As she released his nappy and palpitated his abdomen he gave one tremendous yell. Her fingers registered a hard contraction across his tummy, beneath the surface from left to right, just as she had felt when she'd held him on her shoulder. Then he was sick again, and the same nasty discharge dribbled down his little chin.

Sarah just gazed down at her child with unseeing eyes. Frances picked him up, removed the residue of waste and threw a cloth across her shoulder before she laid the baby's head gently against it. Then she massaged the tiny back until he at last quietened down.

'Sarah, I think it best the doctor takes a look at him,' she said eventually, returning the child to his mother's arms

'But why? It's just sickness, isn't it?'

Frances paused. 'To be honest, I'm not entirely sure. May I ring the surgery?'

Sarah sighed and nodded. 'If you think it's necessary.'

She dialled, knowing for certain now that there was something amiss with both child and mother. But what, she wasn't sure. Bruno came on the line and she briefly explained her misgivings.

'I've two more to see here and then I'll come.' His tone of voice was brisk, but at least he'd registered the urgency of her concern.

Whilst she waited she tried a little conversation. Sarah was wrapped in a world of her own and refused to talk about Freddie. Frances decided to let the subject drop. Obviously she was suffering from some kind of withdrawal from the baby. Perhaps, as Bruno had suggested, it was a case of postnatal depression. But that didn't resolve Freddie's problem. His was definitely biological, she was sure.

When Bruno arrived Sarah left them, going to the kitchen to make coffee.

'Probably better,' he said softly as Frances led the way to the nursery. 'It may upset her to talk about something she refuses to acknowledge.'

Frances picked up Freddie. 'He was sick earlier. I've kept the towel for you to have a look at. But his tummy is what's worrying me. I thought I felt something hard there as it contracted.'

'Colic?'

She hesitated. 'I don't think so. It's like a hard disc moving across his abdomen.'

Bruno nodded. 'Right, young fellow, let's take your temperature and examine you. Can we unbutton this thing?'

Ten minutes later, he supported the child in the crook of his arm. A deep frown was etched into his forehead as he studied the tiny features.

Sarah stood unsurely in the doorway, carrying the drinks on a tray. 'He's all right, isn't he?'

Bruno looked up, his expression concerned. 'Sarah, I want to have this vomiting checked out. I think Freddie needs to be examined by a specialist, and that can only be done at the hospital.'

'Today?'

'Yes. As soon as possible. I'd like to make a call now to arrange it.'

'But my daughter . . . she needs to be collected from school!'

'Could your husband collect her?' Frances suggested gently. 'Or perhaps there's a friend with whom she could stay for a few hours?'

'But I always meet her from school!'

Bruno walked towards her, baby in arms. 'Sarah, this is very important. Freddie must be seen by a paediatrician.'

'Does that mean he's seriously ill?'

He hesitated. 'Until we have clinical tests done, I'm afraid I can't answer that. But I'm sure all of us want to see Freddie better.'

Sarah nodded slowly, looking ashen. Frances took the tray from her whilst Bruno made the necessary arrangements by phone and rang Mr Clark at work on Sarah's behalf, to explain the situation.

He was home within ten minutes. He had been quite unaware that his son was so unwell, and agreed immediately to collect Joanna from school and said that in the meantime he would wait with his wife for the ambulance to arrive.

'What's wrong with Freddie?' Frances asked, once outside.

'I think he has congenital pyloric stenosis.'

Frances nodded. 'I thought it might be. It's a condition which sometimes afflicts first sons, isn't it?'

His dark eyes were impressed. 'That's right. The pylorus connects the stomach to the duodenum, and with this the wall of the pylorus thickens and the passageway inside narrows. As a result the milk can't pass from the stomach to the intestine.'

Frances sighed wearily. 'But that that still doesn't explain his mother's attitude.'

'No, it's a separate issue,' he agreed, glancing at his watch. 'Let's get the baby sorted out, then we'll give some thought to Sarah.'

But it might be too late by then!' Frances protested unhappily. 'How is she going to cope?'

He laid a hand on her shoulder. 'You can't take on everything at once, Frances. She obviously resents being interrogated— and whatever you say now will only seem like an inquisition to her. She'll think you're interfering and she'll resent you for it. When Freddie is better, we'll have more chance of getting to the root of the problem.'

Frances shook her head. 'But what about—?'

'Look,' he interrupted with a deep sigh, 'at the moment I can't think about anything except a ham sandwich with pickle and a long, cool drink. Damn alarm gave up the ghost this morning. I didn't even have time to grab a coffee.'

She couldn't believe it. He was fending her off again! Didn't he understand that Sarah Clark needed help? And not in six months' time, when it would be too late, but now!

She marched after him. 'Dr Quillan!'

He was already moving off in the Range Rover. He saw her wave and stopped. 'What's up now, Frances?'

She thrust her face up at the window. 'You're avoiding me again!'

He frowned and stuck an elbow on the window ledge. 'What on earth do you mean?'

'It seems to me I have to listen when you want to discuss a contentious issue—but there's never time when the situation is reversed!'

He gave her a wry look. 'A contentious issue?'

'Petra Bally,' she retorted swiftly, realising how angry she still felt about it, but wishing at the same time that it hadn't surfaced whilst she was angry.

The engine shuddered. 'Come to the Ferryman. We'll eat and talk at the same time—about all these contentious issues of yours.'

'But I'm not hungry!'

'Well, I'm afraid I am. See you there in five minutes.'

The engine flew into life. She stepped back and watched him roar away. Well, it was either the pub or nothing. She supposed it had better be the pub!

*   *   *

Frances ignored the menu proffered in front of her.

'Choose—or I'll choose for you!'

She blanched under the curious stare of the Ferryman's bar staff 'Tuna sandwich, please,' she agreed lamely.

Two thickly cut ham sandwiches, with lashings of pickle, one tuna sandwich and two cream sodas were duly ordered.

He took her arm and wheeled her to a corner seat. 'Right, spill the beans. What's this about Gabriel Bally?'

It's just that you didn't give me a chance to defend myself,' she said stiffly, clenching her hands in her lap. She felt odd in her uniform, but no one seemed to be looking.

'I wasn't accusing you.'

'Then I must have seriously misunderstood! Your words were that Petra Bally had made a complaint which—'

'Which I had to accept. If I hadn't it would have gone over my head.'

'But there wasn't a shred of truth in her allegation!'

He shrugged. 'Then there's no need for concern, is there?'

'But you said—'

'Look, I merely told you what had

happened. Would you have preferred to find out for yourself—literally walk into a hornets' nest?'

She paused, aware that he had a point. Grudgingly she shook her head.

'OK. What else?'

She snorted. 'Since your time is so precious—'

He leaned forward, lowering his voice: 'Look, what's this bee in your bonnet about my time?'

'Simply . . . that if you had shared a little of it with me in that first week, I would have had something to work on with the patients. For instance Cynthia Vail.'

The food arrived. 'Go on,' he mumbled, lunging into his sandwich.

'Well, Cynthia . . . she isn't easy at the best of times. I could have done with some moral support.'

'Apologies,' he said. 'She is a bit of a stickler, I agree.'

Frances nodded, biting into her own sandwich. She studied him, doubtful whether he agreed at all and wondering if this wasn't going in one ear and out the other. 'Then there is Sarah,' she went on hesitantly. 'She's been distinctly frosty from the start. My approach could have been made so much easier if—'

He held up his hands. 'If I'd pulled my weight?'

She was speechless. 'Exactly!'

95

He scooped up the last few remnants of his sandwich and downed the pint-glass of cream soda. Then he sat back, replete, dabbed his mouth with a napkin and licked his lips. 'Mmm Better. Now, where were we?'

'Sarah Clark?'

'Yes, well done on that. What made you first suspect something was wrong?'

Amazing, she thought, her jaw dropping. Now she felt as though she didn't have a leg to stand on! 'Well . . .' she faltered unsurely, 'I remember in training, we had first-born twins with the same problem. The little hard patch going across Freddie's stomach seemed to give it away. That rang a bell today, and shifted me away from thinking the problem was psychological—between Sarah and Freddie.'

He shrugged. 'Well, it still may be. But I can't do anything for Sarah until she's back in her home environment with the child. Then I'll have a chat with her—I don't want to put her on medication unnecessarily if she can be counselled. And you know yourself that's not going to be achieved in five minutes.'

Frances realised that he was right, and also felt a little guiltily that she had panicked. Her thoughts must have shown on her face because he raised one eyebrow and tutted. 'You didn't think I would just dismiss the depression, did you?'

She shrugged. 'I wasn't sure how you felt about that kind of thing—'

'"That kind of thing"', he said, quietly but emphatically, 'is just as important as a broken limb or a biological disease, and I feel very sympathetic to women who have it—for whatever reason. But I couldn't just go barging in on the Clarks making radical assumptions, and besides, I had every confidence in you.'

'Me?' She stared at him in surprise.

He nodded. 'I trust your judgement—your intuition. And if you look in the appointments diary you'll see I've made a note to call with you again tomorrow morning. The child could have suffered dehydration, and chemical imbalances to the body fluids are extremely serious.'

She felt a tinge of pink in her cheeks. 'I . . . didn't look.'

He shrugged. 'Well, none of us are perfect, are we?'

This time she went bright red. She should have checked. First rule of the morning—always look in the book and review the appointments.

'Anyway,' he said, watching her, 'we'll wait now until we discover what happens with Freddie, and then we'll treat the remainder of the problem when he's back home and Sarah has one less problem to deal with.'

She nodded slowly. 'I suppose it is pyloric stenosis?'

'I'm as certain as I can be.'

Frances sighed. 'Poor little chap.'

Bruno smiled ruefully and his brown eyes deepened in colour. 'Smitten, are you?'

She glanced up at him sharply. 'Most women have the maternal instinct—'

'And you, Frances,' he interrupted softly, 'have you?'

'I'm not even married!' she burst out, gulping down her drink, avoiding his gaze.

He laughed. 'And you believe in the institution?'

'Of course I do!' She stared at him with startled blue eyes. 'Children need a mother and a father and security, and only marriage can offer that in my personal opinion . . .'

'Indeed?' he mused, crossing one long leg and wiggling his toes perilously near her calf 'Refreshing . . . though perhaps not a popular opinion these days.'

She moved her leg. 'I've never held with doing or agreeing with things because they were popular, and I've seen enough of dysfunctional families in the army to know I don't want one. Thank God, my parents loved each other and are still together, and my brothers are both married and happily settled, but I think it's basically down to the woman in the beginning. If she settles for less than she believes in, she's not being honest and—' Suddenly she stopped, realising that she was pouring out her heart and that he had managed to make her do it—all in the space of five minutes.

'Don't stop,' he murmured softly, and she felt a wash of warmth run up from her toes to her hairline.

'We are supposed to be talking about work!' she protested angrily, cross with herself for being diverted.

'But this is much more interesting.' He sighed as he looked at her resolute face and her small shoulders suddenly squared as if for a fight. 'Oh, Frances, you're such a temptation to tease.'

Anger and embarrassment made her snap open her mouth to respond, but he forestalled her by standing up and holding out his hand as he gave her a rueful grin. 'Come on, then,' he laughed. 'Enough for one day.' He looked at her wryly, and as she glared at him muttered drily, 'After all, time is precious and we shouldn't waste it by enjoying ourselves!'

*　　*　　*

Thanks to Louise Lambert, the health visitor, Frances managed to trim her afternoon down a little, which she could well do with after lunch in the Ferryman. At least a direction on Sarah Clark had been resolved, but she'd had to endure the indignity of being mocked to achieve it. Damn the man. Somehow he always got to her, and she responded—usually by feeling humiliated and annoyed. They hadn't even got around to the Ballys, and by now she was beginning to think a confrontation was hardly worth the torment.

Louise had already called in once to see Cynthia, who still had a nutrition problem. Her condition had been discovered at Christmas, when she had been found hypothermic by a neighbour and delivered to hospital over the festive season.

Bruno reported that she had been back home in January but that he was concerned about her frailty, and he had asked Benita to check her frequently. However, Cynthia was also stubborn and independent, and she didn't like changes. Benita had tried to persuade her to have meals delivered, said the notes, but to no avail. If Louise had not finally managed to convince her that meals on wheels and attendance at luncheon clubs were not catches but worthwhile options for survival, then Frances would have had a tough time indeed. Here was another occasion on which she could have employed the GP's help—if he'd been available to offer it!

She noticed, in Cynthia's careplan, that Nigel Drew had attended her whilst he was on call last week and had asked for an iron injection to be given after the results of her full blood count.

When she arrived Frances cautiously approached the subject and was flatly refused.

It was Cynthia's soap day, and an Australian saga on TV was switched on at full-blast.

Bowing to cowardice, Frances gave up and arranged to do it later in the week.

She flew through her three remaining calls—two diabetic checks and a post-op call—and went home for a long, cool soak in the bath, trying not to harbour resentfulness that Bruno hadn't kept a firmer hand on the elderly lady who made everyone's life so difficult. He was, after all, supposed to be her GP!

                    *   *   *

It had turned into a glorious June.

Frances knocked at Cynthia Vail's door a few days later and felt the heat rebound from the white paintwork.

Cynthia welcomed her gloomily. 'Iron injection, is it, missy?'

'Something to give you a bit of a boost,' she said with a smile. 'All right to do it now?'

'As right as I'll ever be. Come on in, then.'

She followed her through, familiar now with the tiny house, sparsely furnished but sunny, as it faced south and overlooked a small patch of garden. The elderly lady sank into an armchair. 'Where's that doctor of yours today?'

Frances lowered her case to the table. 'Nigel Drew?'

Cynthia tutted. 'Not him. The other one. The one with the brown eyes.'

Frances didn't look up, but she knew that

101

Cynthia was staring at her. 'Dr Quillan?' she asked matter-of-factly.

'That's him. Got a little boy, hasn't he? Left a widower. Had all that trouble with his wife. And if I'm not much mistaken she looked a fair bit like you.'

Frances was speechless for a moment. Just who in this town wasn't aware of the fact? 'Sit back, please,' she said sharply, determinedly avoiding Cynthia's laser gaze. 'Now just try to relax.'

The application, because it involved moving the subcutaneous layer of skin to one side before injecting the iron-dextran, was known as a Z-shaped injection, and Cynthia glowered at her as she leant over. 'All this palaver. Don't see why I should have to bother,' her patient complained ungratefully.

'Well, you don't want to keep feeling tired and run-down, do you? Your anaemia won't get any better by itself. Which reminds me, are you keeping to your diet plan?'

'Can't do otherwise with all you lot pestering. me. Ouch!'

'Just a second more. Fine—that's it, all over.'

Frances dabbed the spot with cotton wool and tidied away, relieved that she hadn't encountered more of a running battle.

'And what about that other doctor—the lady? The one who had the rumpus with her husband? Better than watching soap operas it is, when I hear all that goes on at that surgery of yours.'

'And just how do you hear?' Frances asked with a frown.

'You may well ask. Just let's say I'm not as daft as I looks.'

'I never thought you were, Cynthia!'

Frances decided to end the conversation there. The fact that everyone seemed to know the practice business filled her with dismay. And that remark about Lindsay—what was it? 'All that trouble with his wife'? Well, there was no way she was going to be drawn into gossip, although she would have to make it quite plain to one and all that she had absolutely no intention of trying to fill the first Mrs Quillan's shoes!

Cynthia pulled back her shoulders and sat upright. 'I don't repeat a word, mind. I just listens and takes it all in and keeps it to myself.' She tapped her long, thin nose.

Frances sighed and gave up. 'Since I'm here we'll have a look at those feet of yours with the long nails and then your gums. Dr Drew has written in your notes that you had an infection around those bottom teeth. Cleared up, has it?'

'As far as I know.' Grumbling again, the old woman submitted to Frances's ministrations. Her buccal mucosa seemed to have cleared with the mouthwash that Nigel had prescribed and, whilst she had her in an obliging mood,

Frances also gave her an ear syringing—made easier by the oil that Cynthia had reluctantly applied over the past week. Not that Cynthia was hard of hearing by her accounts of what she'd gleaned from this mysterious grapevine.

Even so, Frances felt sorry for her, and tried to engage in less lethal conversation than tearing the surgery staff to pieces. But it seemed that she knew quite a lot about the practice, even down to the receptionists' names. And that was a surprise as she had never visited the surgery in person.

When Frances had concluded her visit she promised to call again in a week, and then she remembered that she still had Richard Grove to visit and the afternoon was half way through already.

As she was going past Bow Lane she couldn't resist popping in. Her small garden lawn was smattered with pink and white clover and a marmalade cat pounced on unsuspecting wasps as they hovered over the yellow hearts of the daisies. Rolling in an eiderdown of sticky purple vetch, he shook himself free and spat at the angry insect.

Absorbed in her window reverie, she jumped as the phone rang and hurried to answer it.

'Fran? Can you come over this weekend? Grandma says it's all right.' It was Jack, unceremoniously getting straight to the point.

'Your grandmother might have other plans,'

she prevaricated.

'No, she says she hasn't. I asked her first.'

'Jack . . . I . . .'

'She likes you coming. She s-says to c-come and have lunch on Saturday.'

The stutter again. He was agitated, probably because he was afraid she'd refuse, and, more to put him at ease than anything else, she agreed. Oh, what a weak will, she rebuked herself, staring at the phone. Would Bruno be there? Could she avoid him? Perhaps if she went early in the morning then she could escape before lunch and give apologies that she had to eat somewhere else. It might work. Besides, Rosa had said that he was hardly ever home on a Saturday . . .

For some reason Suzie Collins sprang to mind. Probably because she'd seen her name down on the rota for Saturday morning emergency surgery. Silly. She'd even furtively watched Suzie Collins, watched Bruno's eyes and mouth and body language as he spoke to her. But although Suzie had seemed engrossed in just looking at him, he hadn't seemed to respond—and anyway, what about Meg Fellows? Wasn't she more on Bruno's social level? Plus she was divorced . . .

Oh, heaven help me, she thought as she marked the Saturday off on her calendar. What an idiot I am. For heaven's sake, you don't even like the man and here you are letting him run rampant in your thoughts!

Shaking her head as if to clear it, she glanced in the mirror before she left for Richard Grove's. Her hair was piled high into a golden knot and she tidied her fringe, which needed a trim and danced occasionally in her eyes. The sun had caught her face and arms and she was a tawny, creamy colour now, which made her eyes seem a melting cornflower-blue. Pressing her dress over her small breasts and tucking her belt down, she dabbed a touch of Estee behind her ears.

When she arrived at the Groves' sumptuous house, with a shock she saw the Range Rover. Too late. She couldn't reverse without being seen. She took a steadying breath.

Gwen Grove opened the door to her and waved her in. And what was she thinking about anyway? Hadn't she been harping on enough about his unavailability? Perhaps he'd checked on her visits and had decided, after the session in the Ferryman, that he would make an effort to appease her and meet her halfway with the patients?

Well, if that was the case, she must have got through . . . at last.

It was a notion she was soon to dismiss when she saw Richard Grove and Bruno Quillan relaxed in sun loungers, drinks in hand, sharing a joke which almost brought the house down.

CHAPTER FIVE

Bruno smiled and stood up. 'I didn't know you were calling today.'

She glanced at him, trying to look as though it were the most natural thing in the world to have arrived at the same time as the GP. 'Er . . . thought I'd better check, since Mr Grove was wiggling that suspect finger rather dangerously last time I came,' she returned lightly.

Richard Grove laughed. 'Your nurse doesn't trust me, Bruno.'

'And neither do I!' Bruno pulled out a chair for her.

They caught each other's glance.

'Here it is, then,' the builder said, heaving himself up and planting his hand on the table. 'Do your worst, the pair of you.'

Frances spread out her sterile sheet and dressings and slipped on her gloves. Bruno examined the finger after she had removed the old dressing and gave a nod. 'Not too bad. How's the range of movement?'

'Could be better. But then I'm of the belief that fresh air cures all. With these darned bandages around me, I'll never heal.' His patient lifted each finger slowly. Around the wound where the tight synovium had been surgically straightened there was a suspicious streak of inflammation.

'Right. I'll let Sister Duncan clean and dress it, but I'm afraid you're going to have to keep it under wraps for a bit longer. And I'm going to give you an antibiotic—which I want you to take and not keep in a cupboard somewhere!'

The man groaned. His wife chuckled as she bent over to have a look. 'That'll teach you to boast you haven't had a day off from work in years.'

'I seem to be making up for lost time,' her husband complained, unamused, and Frances left them to it, finding her way to the kitchen to throw away the soiled detritus.

She ran her hands under the tap and soaped them, and was soon joined by Gwen, who sighed noisily.

'Men! I'll be glad when he's out from under my feet, to be honest. Talk about making a bad patient!' She gave Frances a lingering glance as she poured lemonade into a jug. 'Bruno tells us Jack is going to Harrington Hall in September?'

Frances looked up from drying her hands. 'Yes . . . yes, I believe so.'

'I hear Jack's taken quite a shine to you.'

Frances stiffened. Was this about to be a repeat of Cynthia Vail's observations? She'd forgotten just how quickly news travelled in close communities, yet she was beginning to wonder if Bruno himself had elaborated in this case—the Groves appeared to be friends of his—although, ironically, Bruno was the one person who hadn't remarked on her similarity to Lindsay . . . yet.

'Carl, our son, is just a year older than Jack,' Gwen chattered on. 'They went to the primary together, although Carl was always one class ahead of Jack. Richard and Bruno used to bump into each other regularly at football matches. That's how they first got to know each other. Shame about his wife. We never met her. And he's never talked about her either . . .'

Frances expelled a sigh, ignoring the twinge of guilt she had for suspecting Bruno of gossip. She met Gwen's probing little eyes and vowed silently that she would not respond to the woman's blatant attempt at fishing. Instead, she continued to dry her hands.

'Pity about Jack's asthma,' remarked Gwen. 'He always wound up in the reserves. Never mind, Harrington Hall will toughen him up. Carl's in the rugby squad already.'

Frances shuddered at the thought of Jack being toughened up. Why did people always assume that all that was needed to make a boy a man was a speedy initiation into sweaty football shirts and cold showers?

'Harrington Hall will be the answer for Jack.' Richard Grove was continuing in the same vein as he walked in. 'Nothing like a public school education to knock the rough edges into shape!'

109

Frances stole a glance at Bruno's face. She was sure he avoided looking at her. More than relieved when the drinks had been drunk and their goodbyes said, they walked together to the cars in silence.

He said suddenly, 'It'll be handy for Jack to have a friend there—at Harrington Hall.'

'A friend?' She answered more sharply than she had meant. 'I didn't realise Jack and Carl were close.'

'No, not exactly close.' He laid a hand on her arm and she looked up. 'Gwen and Richard mean well. They're just a bit OTT when it comes to Carl.'

She shrugged. 'He's obviously the type of boy who is cut out for rugger scrums.'

'And Jack isn't?' The sun was warm in a mellowing sky, and his eyes reflected the depth of colour that seemed to fill the June day.

'I would say Jack has other skills.'

'Yes,' he agreed, 'he has. And sending him to Harrington Hall is a decision I didn't make lightly. Heaven knows, he's my only son and I care deeply about him But perhaps that's precisely the reason he needs a damn good education.'

'Which you feel he wouldn't receive at a state school?'

'I'm not suggesting he wouldn't receive an adequate education, but with boarding there would be more time—'

'Exactly. Isn't time what this is really about?

If Lindsay were still alive would you still be sending him away?'

He stiffened. 'That's an unfair question.'

'Is it?' She sighed. 'Look, this is getting us nowhere. You really shouldn't lead me into discussions over Jack—your mind is already made up.'

He stopped her as she turned away. 'I'm only trying to do what's best for the lad—you understand that, don't you?'

Those words made her cringe. She had heard them enough in her own life, when adults had always seemed to attach them to unpalatable decisions. She had been unable to argue with army life or its disciplines, and luckily she hadn't come off too badly—but that was because she had been resilient enough to stand up for herself. Not so Jack, she felt, who was not only an especially sensitive child, but who had also had the trauma of losing one parent. In a sense he would be losing another.

Bruno sighed wearily and a wave of sympathy washed over her. Being a doctor tested all one's values—she understood that. The medical profession was not an easy life by any standards, especially in today's social environment. But was that sufficient reason to make such a radical decision on Jack's future?

'When do you want me to see Mr Grove next?' she asked, changing the subject deliberately.

He looked at her for a long while before

111

answering, and then, shrugging, he glanced back at the house. 'Better be the day after tomorrow. He'll want fresh dressings then.'

'Fine.' She looked up at him and smiled. 'See you back at the surgery.'

He nodded, and she jumped into the Clio and started the engine. Hauling the wheel around and circling the Range Rover, she drove away, vowing that that was the last time she would be drawn into the subject of Jack—or Lindsay—again.

Lunch with Rosa and Jack.

Again, it was a magnificent day, and Rosa had set lunch in the conservatory, where the tubs of flowers were brimming with life. She caught Rosa's eye and the wistful smile on her face as she dished out buttered new potatoes.

Jack glanced at Frances. 'Did you know people are always more ill at the weekend or right in the middle of the night?'

Rosa and Frances laughed, catching one another's eye again. 'I'm not surprised,' Frances chuckled. 'But how do you know that?'

He shrugged as he lunged into his food, reminding Frances of a certain other appetite. 'Well, we used to have picnics and things like that in summer, but we never have them any more,' he said simply, 'and I wake up hearing Dad go out more in the nights now.'

At this piece of logic Frances felt her throat tighten, and she glanced again at Rosa, whose smile had evaporated.

'Have you told Frances about going to Christina's?' Rosa asked quickly . . .'

Jack shook his head. 'I visit my aunt Christina in Brighton every year in the summer holidays. All together I've got one aunt and one uncle. But my uncle Graham is in New Zealand, so we don't see much of him. I've got two cousins there, Karen and James, and they might be coming over next year to see us. Or, if not, we might be going to them, mightn't we, Grandma?'

Rosa nodded. 'Perhaps. We'll have to wait and see. It all depends on your father's schedule.'

Meal demolished, Jack scraped back his chair. 'Can I take Fran up to my room now?'

Rosa gasped in horror. 'She hasn't even begun her soup!'

Frances grinned. 'I'll not be long. Jack, why don't you go ahead and set the computer up?'

He didn't need telling twice, and Rosa shook her head in exasperation as he bolted from the, table. 'He can't sit still for five minutes. That blessed machine upstairs is all he thinks of '

'Well, it's a good thing in a way. All the schools have computer facilities now. In a few years educational books will be a thing of the past.'

Rosa nodded and at back. 'So Christina tells me. She's a computer analyst for a large industrial company. To be honest, I don't understand a word she says.'

Frances set down her spoon. 'Jack must be in his element, then, when he stays with her.'

Rosa studied her carefully. 'Yes, she tries to occupy him as best she can. Christina and her husband Nigel are in their mid-thirties and deliberately opted not to have children. Lindsay wasn't maternal either. I think, she gave Bruno a child just to please him. Motherhood was . . . not a natural state for her to be in.'

Frances looked up sharply. 'Lindsay and Christina are sisters—your daughters?'

'Didn't you know?'

Frances slowly shook her head, astounded. She had assumed, because Bruno and Rosa seemed so close, that they were the blood-related ones.

'You thought Bruno was my son?'

Frances flushed, feeling ridiculous. 'I . . . yes, I suppose I did. I really didn't give it much thought.'

Rosa smiled and shrugged it off. 'I'm afraid Bruno's own parents died. His mother shortly followed his father about four years ago, and Graham, Bruno's brother, is older than Bruno by two years—thirty-eight. He decided to move out to New Zealand, where he bought a farm. A pity, really, because Karen and James are near Jack's age and his only cousins.' She smiled sympathetically. 'You and Bruno

114

haven't had much time to get to know one another, have you?'

Frances took a breath, still trying to get over the assumption, the very wrong one she had made, that Bruno was Rosa's son. 'No . . . No . . .' She flushed as she saw the curious expression on the older woman's face. 'A doctor doesn't need to know much about his nurse or vice versa—and I am only temporary . . . very temporary at the surgery.'

'But I thought you two were getting along so well?' She looked crestfallen. 'You must forgive me, my dear, I seem to have been labouring under a misunderstanding too.' She sat forward and clasped her hands on the table, looking levelly into Frances's eyes. 'Bruno is sometimes deceiving . . . a bit brusque . . . sometimes even off-hand. He's been like that since . . . Lindsay's death. I feel it's a protective skin he girds about him.'

Comments which Frances pondered on, despite the level of concentration she had to muster for the computer games Jack showed her. What had Rosa meant about labouring under a misunderstanding? she wondered as the screen of the computer played colourful graphic scenes of endangered species.

She remained with Jack for a while, and Rosa insisted she stay for tea, but instead she offered to take Jack to the flat, where she could relax without worrying about Bruno returning home. It would also allow Rosa

115

a few hours of gardening peace. Everyone seemed happy with the suggestion, and for the next couple of hours Jack helped her in her own little garden back at Bow Lane.

Bruno had been home and eaten by the time she dropped Jack back. A call had taken him out minutes before they arrived.

'Will you come next weekend?' Jack stood solemnly at the front door as she left.

Rosa interrupted swiftly. 'Frances has other things to do, dear. We've occupied enough of her time already.'

Seeing the obvious disappointment on the boy's face, and his tiny, drooping shoulders, Frances hesitated. 'Well . . . what about a picnic, if you haven't had one for ages—the three of us?'

'Ace!' Jack's blue eyes lit up and he hurtled forward and threw his arms up and around her neck.

Frances guiltily felt herself hugging him back, the skinny little frame beneath her hands seemingly so receptive to affection.

'If you're sure?' Rosa agreed, and looked at Frances questioningly.

She nodded. 'I'll ring to confirm.'

Rosa smiled. 'I'll cook a chicken and we can have it cold.'

They both looked down at Jack as he said, 'And I'll ask Dad if he can come too.'

Rosa bit her lip. 'Better not worry him, darling, not just yet. He is terribly busy at the moment. Some other time, perhaps.'

Frances glanced at her gratefully, then added, 'You never know, the weather might not be kind either . . . we might have to cancel at the last moment. So don't get your hopes too high!'

*   *   *

Gill passed the phone to Frances on Friday afternoon, her eyebrows arched in question.

'For you or Dr Quillan.'

'Who is it?' Frances took the receiver, covering the mouthpiece with her hand.

'Madjur Rasti. Sounds dreadful.'

'Where's Dr Quillan?'

The receptionist checked the diary at the desk. 'He'll be halfway through his calls by now. Do you want me to page him?'

Frances hesitated, then shook her head.

'Madjur? This is Frances Duncan.'

The weak voice on the end of the line was a disorientated mumble.

'Madjur, I'm coming over straight away. Leave the door open if you can.'

Heart racing, Frances gathered her case and bent over Gill at her desk. 'I've changed my mind, Gill. Madjur Rasti does sound ill. Can you ring Dr Quillan and tell him I've gone over there?'

Gill nodded and picked up the phone.

Because of busy roads, it was almost fifteen

minutes before she found herself at the house. The door wasn't open, and though she looked in the window, she couldn't see anyone. Then she went to the back garden and tried the kitchen door. Luckily it was open and she walked in, aware of a smothering sense of depression hanging over the house.

'Madjur?' she called.

There was no reply and she called again. 'In here,' sobbed a voice, and Frances ran into the lounge.

She found her lying on the floor by the window, her coal-black eyes red-veined and her cheeks puffy with weeping. 'Madjur? What's happened? Did you fall?'

Tears began to run in silent rivulets down her cheeks. 'My legs gave way: I can't support myself.'

Frances knelt beside her and propped her up so that she leaned into her chest. 'Did you hurt yourself?'

'I . . . I don't think so.'

'Don't worry, Dr Quillan's on his way.'

'I'm sorry . . .'

'There's nothing to be sorry for. Now, I wonder if we can get you to the couch?'

Madjur winced as in slow stages and with Frances's help she moved to the bed-settee. Frances lifted her housecoat to examine the knee 'Oh, Madjur, you can't go on like this. Something will have to be done.' She sighed as she saw the grotesquely swollen joints—on both knees this time.

A fresh rush of tears engulfed the woman as Bruno made his way in through the kitchen entrance.

His soft brown eyes seemed to take in the situation at once, and he came over and pulled up a chair. 'Nothing broken?' he asked in a quiet voice.

'Not broken,' Frances confirmed, 'but very swollen.'

He gave her a thorough examination. 'Madjur, there is absolutely no alternative,' he said after a while. 'You must have this bursa attended to at the very least. I'm going to draw the fluid off the right knee for now, but then I'm going to find a bed for you in hospital.'

Fearing another refusal, Frances braced herself for the worst. But Madjur had obviously reached the end of her endurance, and just turned her head into the pillow.

Bruno spread his case out on the table and was preparing the needle and syringe as Frances went to help him, taking a pack of sterile cloths and donning gloves. She glanced up and asked hesitantly, 'Do you think she'll go?'

His face was set. 'There is a limit to unnecessary suffering. And I think she's come to it.'

'Will you be able to get her in at such short notice?'

'I'm going to have a damn good try. This is

what fund-holding is supposed to be about!' he muttered grimly 'Getting the best health service for your patient in the swiftest possible time. And by God, I'm going to move heaven and earth to see she has it.'

The painful procedure was undertaken yet again, and Frances realised that Madjur had no energy left to argue. When Bruno had drawn off as much fluid from her knee as he could, she bandaged the joint and eased her knees onto a pillow.

'I'm going to, make you tea,' she said softly as Bruno disappeared, and she heard the click of the phone in the hall.

Madjur nodded, seeming to have given up on the fight. Her eyes were so swollen that she could hardly see out of them.

Frances listened to Bruno's deep, firm voice. She didn't relish the job of the poor secretary on the other end of the phone, who was obviously trying to cover for her boss. But at last the calls ended and Bruno walked back into the room.,

'I've found a bed in Stillerton General,' he told them. 'Now, don't look so worried, Madjur. Ben Carter is a friend of mine and he's a very fine doctor. I've impressed on him that you've had a lot of pain and he's going to take a good look at your neck— your most recent problem. If your two top vertebrae are badly weakened then we'll need to do something about it. And because the rheumatoid arthritis can affect small arteries, we have to take into consideration your circulation.'

His patient said nothing. She looked awful, and Frances held her hand again and sat beside her, coaxing her to drink the tea.

'I'll stay until the ambulance comes,' she said, and looked up at Bruno. 'I only had one more call, and that was the diabetes case you asked me to check on today.'

Bruno packed his case and smiled down at them. 'I'll call on my way back. It was just a urine test for sugar I wanted—no problem.'

Frances nodded. 'Thanks.'

'I'll just see Dr Quillan to the door, Madjur. Drink the tea, now.'

She left her sipping slowly and went with Bruno along the hall. Much to her surprise, when they were out of earshot, he lowered his voice. 'Don't let Madjur change her mind, whatever happens. Will you be able to manage?'

She nodded and smiled at him with her eyes. 'Yes . . . yes, thanks. I don't think there will be a problem now.'

'You did absolutely the right thing in calling me. I feel we've caught her at the right time— she badly needs reassessment.'

Frances nodded and found herself smiling up into the concerned face. 'Don't worry. I'll see she goes.'

'Good girl.' He turned and was about to

hurry away, and then stopped sharply. 'Oh, by the way, I heard from Dorchester Hospital this morning. Freddie Clark had his op for pyloric stenosis. He'll be home next week, barring any problems. I thought then we'd have a crack at sorting out something for Sarah. Maybe you could look in and check them and I'll follow up, so she doesn't feel bombarded with us both at once?'

'Yes,' Frances agreed at once. 'If you'll make a note in the DN's book when Freddie's home?'

He nodded and grinned. 'Hope the weather's fine tomorrow!' And then he rushed off, long legs carrying him swiftly to the Range Rover. Her eye was caught by the swaying broad shoulders, the casual strength that emanated from his movements and the lovely dark hair curling over his shirt collar—earth-brown against vivid white. And, of course, the aroma lingering in the air after him as he went—which, whether she liked it or not, did the strangest of things to her stomach, giving it a little tumble as she stood on the doorstep.

He crouched over the wheel and turned to glance at her. Quickly she closed the door and took a breath. What was happening? They had actually been civil to one another and had agreed on everything this morning. He'd come immediately to Madjur and treated her compassionately but firmly. No doctor could have done more.

Thoughtful, she walked slowly back in to Madjur. 'How's it going?' she asked gently, and sat beside her on the edge of the bed-settee.

Madjur was too full up with emotion to reply.

Frances squeezed her hand. 'Let me go and pack a bag for you. Shall I just go upstairs and collect what I think is necessary?'

Madjur made a brave effort to smile, and Frances gently wiped her hot cheeks with a tissue and pressed a clean one into her hand. Then she went upstairs, discovered Madjur's bedroom and packed a nightie, robe and slippers in a hold-all she found in the wardrobe. There was a photo beside the bed in a small white frame—it was Madjur . . . except the smaller features and vivid dark eyes told Frances that this was her daughter. She tucked it in the bag and then collected an assortment of things from the bathroom.

At last, downstairs, she sat beside the woman and tried to put her mind at rest by telling her a little about the hospital. After hesitating, she thought to mention that she had enclosed the photo in the bag.

Tears filled Madjur's eyes once again. 'Thank you. It's my daughter, Serena. She's almost sixteen now. She lives in Delhi with her grandparents.'

Frances smiled. 'She's lovely—very much like you.'

Madjur nodded. 'I miss her.'

'Does she know you're sick?'

'No . . . no, I can't write properly with my fingers. And besides . . . I don't want to worry her.'

'But she might worry all the same, not hearing from you.' An idea sprang to Frances's mind. 'I'll write for you, if you like. I could, explain I am your nurse and that since you can't write you would like me to send some news and your love.'

Madjur looked uncertain, but Frances was sure that the idea appealed to her. Then, at the sound of the ambulance coming to a halt outside, Madjur gave in. 'Would you really?'

'Of course. Have you the address?'

'There, in the book by the phone, under S for Serena.'

Frances nodded. 'OK. I'll take it with me after I've seen you off. Is there anything you would like me to do?'

'Just make sure the house is locked and everything is turned off—that's all.' Madjur looked up from under her wet lashes. 'And thank you, Frances. I don't know what I would have done without you today.'

Frances bent and kissed her on the cheek before the ambulancemen came in. Then, when they had finally lifted her on board, she checked the house and wrote Serena's address in her notebook. Pulling the front door after her, she gave a sigh. Why was it that some of the nicest people in the world were so afflicted? Madjur deserved just a little bit of happiness . . . and yet she was so alone.

*   *   *

There was no controversy over the weather!

The Saturday was bright and sunny and windless—a real summer's day. Frances packed cold meats, salad, fruit and cold drinks, and splashed out on a toffee cake as she passed through the town. Jack was waiting at the entrance of the strawberry-pink house, unable to disguise his anticipation as he waved her down the moment the Clio's wheels touched the sandy drive. He tugged open the passenger door and slid in, and with him chattering away she drove up to the front door.

She was so absorbed that she barely saw the figure emerge. Her eyes told her that it was Bruno, but her brain refused to admit the truth of her discovery—which was that he carried a rucksack and had lowered a picnic hamper to the ground beside a beach bag. He looked up and waved.

'Your father's home?' she found herself gasping.

Jack nodded, halfway out of the car. 'Grandma has got a cold, so Dad's coming instead. Grandma managed to cook the chicken last night—but we couldn't find the thermos for drinks.'

The news hit her like a brick, and she gulped. 'A cold?'

'Or flu.'

Jack didn't wait to tell her any more, but bounded over to his father.

This was her nightmare coming true! But why hadn't Rosa phoned her last night and cancelled? Rosa understood the situation—she'd thought.

Her question was soon answered as she climbed out of the Clio and approached Bruno bending over the bags.

'Hi! You'll have to make do with me today. Rosa fell prey to a cold last night and went to bed early, hoping she'd be well enough this morning. But I'm afraid she's worse.' He straightened up and gave her an apologetic shrug.

Frances tried to think of an excuse. 'Shouldn't one of us stay with her?'

'I've suggested that. She won't hear of it. Go try for yourself, if you like—although she's pretty sleepy. A bowl of friar's balsam and two paracetamol seem to have done the trick.'

'Oh, well . . . if she's resting . . .'

Bruno gave her an amused frown. 'Take Jack on your own, if you prefer. I can always go into surgery and relieve Tristan, who is standing in for me.'

She couldn't agree to that! Jack was in his element and would be unbearably disappointed if his father opted out. 'Well,

126

I suppose . . .' she sighed, and looked up to a rueful smile

'Shall we take the Range Rover? There's more room for all this stuff.'

Jack whooped, shouting that he'd bring his kite.

'Cheer up,' Bruno said, smiling like a Cheshire cat, 'I could surprise you. You might enjoy my company.'

She smiled wryly. 'Might I?'

He laughed. 'I honestly didn't plan this. Rosa managed to catch her cold all by herself.'

Still gravely suspicious, Frances sighed. There was nothing for it, she supposed, but to give in.

Intending to make sure that Rosa was comfortable, Frances tiptoed through the hall and into the granny annexe. It was a light and spacious hallway, and the first door on the right was open. She poked her head around and saw Rosa, fast asleep in bed.

On her way out; Bruno met her. 'Do you believe me now?'

She gathered the rugs in her arms and quirked an eyebrow.

Eventually, with all the goodies transferred from the Clio into the Range Rover, they set off.

Her eyes strayed several times to the disturbing figure of Bruno in the driver's seat beside her, and the cool blue T-shirt and Bermuda shorts he wore. He seemed to fill them out in all the right places—depressingly healthy muscles protruding from the short sleeves, and thighs so hard-looking and bronzed as they moved to change gear that she swung her head back to the road and told herself that she must be a sex-starved fool for thinking the thoughts she was thinking!

Jack had his headphones on in the back, singing along with his favourite pop tunes. Bruno glanced across and smiled at her. Her heart seemed to crash in time with the engine—a percussion beat all of its own. But why?

Bruno Quillan meant nothing to her. She could take his mockery and his teasing all in her stride if she just kept her cool. Anyway, Jack was there. Nothing could happen with Jack around, could it?

She flushed. She leant further back. She breathed deeply.

And she kept her gaze firmly on the road.

*   *   *

At least she had worn the right clothes: shorts, which were not too short, and camel-coloured, which wouldn't show the dirt—and there was plenty of it around, she espied as they arrived in the wooded glen—a tie-waist blouse in a pretty soft pink and a chiffon scarf in the same hue wrapped around her head to keep back her long fawn hair. She'd chosen tan

128

espadrilles to complement the shorts, avoiding trainers as it was so hot. As she jumped down from the Range Rover it was obvious that Bruno was staring at her with frank appraisal, his eyes following the curve of her long, shapely legs.

Startled, she began to wonder if shorts had been such a good idea . . .

'Cricket first?' yelled Jack, so ebullient that he'd quite forgotten the unpacking.

Bruno wrenched his gaze from her legs. 'Let's put the gear out first, then we'll have a game.'

'Barrier cream for the sun,' Frances admonished, and waylaid Jack and rubbed the cream in over his legs and arms. He giggled as he stood still long enough for her to complete a fairly comprehensive covering of freckled skin.

'Cricketers always have those white pads over their noses,' she told him as she stood up and pulled a baseball cap over his blond head. 'But I suppose we'll let you off for today.'

She could see that he enjoyed the attention. His blue eyes came up and her heart gave a little twist.

'I'll practise while I wait!' he yelled, blushing, and they laughed as they watched him run off through the trees and onto the green.

'And what about me?' Bruno grinned. He pulled the blue T-shirt over his head. 'I'm extremely sensitive to the sun!'

She almost toppled over. The shock of seeing him half naked suddenly, right before her eyes, took all her breath away. A broad chest covered in wiry dark hair met her eyes; she could see the tight, sharp muscle beneath, and the flat abdomen, with its spear of dark hair vanishing just below the waistline of the blue Bermudas.

'Something wrong?' Bruno grinned, unashamedly standing so close that she could feel his breath on her face.

Her chaperon, Jack, had traitorously disappeared.

They were alone!

'N-nothing's wrong!' She pushed the tube or sunscreen at him. 'Here, do it yourself!'

He laughed. 'Now, that's not very nice. What if I get burnt? Look, there are some parts I can't reach.' He raised a long brown arm and patted his back, teasing her with his dark eyes.

She snapped, 'Then you'll have to burn, won't you? Or put that thing back on! Anyway, you look as if you're the last person on earth who would burn!'

He eyed the discarded T-shirt. 'Ah, but I get very hot when I work physically.'

Ignoring the innuendo, she lifted her chin 'I do too, but I keep my clothes on!'

He made a face. 'More's the pity. Shall I rub some on the parts which aren't to be secreted?'

'You're really enjoying all this, aren't you?' she demanded on a gasp. 'And if it wasn't for the fact that I actually saw Rosa in bed, I wouldn't have been surprised if you'd manipulated all this just to . . . just to—'

'Just to what?' He grinned at her wickedly. 'Have my wicked way with you—alone in the forest?' He laughed. 'I think you're perfectly safe here, with young Tiger on the prowl—and anyway, I'm on my best behaviour today.'

'You'd better be!' She pushed him away, stuck her head in the back of the Range Rover and began to haul out the hamper, her cheeks burning as she felt a deep flush cover them. luckily hidden from his obvious delight in being able to tease her so easily.

'Need any help?'

'No . . . thank you.'

But she got stuck. The hamper was heavy and she couldn't quite nudge it out of the gap it was in. He put large brown hands over hers and took it from her, so she was squashed against the chassis, her bottom up against the paintwork, no escape either way. She couldn't have moved, however, for the blood in her legs had turned to water as she stared up at the deliciously open lips, smiling . . . inviting, oh, so inviting. And then those lips were on hers. She wriggled a little until she heard the hamper clunk on the earth and then felt her whole world turn upside down as she slid her hand around a strong neck and closed her eyes.

It was an incredible kiss.

Soft and smooth, turning to hard and powerful, sending her brain reeling as he entered her mouth with his tongue like before—like the night in the garden. And all at once she wasn't just a mere recipient; her fingers were cooperating, threading up into the hair which the realised she'd longed to touch again, to feel, to knead between her fingerpads. Which she did all the more as the kiss went on. And then his hand went down to her hips, and lower, to pull her in, and the heat of their touching bodies seemed to blow her mind.

Until a child's voice echoed in the distance and warning bells sounded, and Bruno broke from her and she swirled in a daze and reached out to steady herself.

CHAPTER SIX

Jack bounced around the door of the Range Rover.

'Can we fly the kite first?' he yelled, and Frances went onto automatic pilot as she tried to steady her nerves, turning her back, pretending to unravel the rugs as Bruno responded to Jack.

She had no idea how long they had been

linked together, only that she had been indulging herself in the pleasure of being kissed. But she didn't like Bruno Quillan, did she? That was the point!

She kept her head down, sure that Jack would notice if she looked at him. Her lips were throbbing from that kiss. As she ran her tongue over them she remembered doing the same the first time he had kissed her, the night in the garden—and now she had let it happen again, and this time nearly in front of Jack.

She was mortified. And his father should have known better—though he probably thought it all very amusing!

'Take the kite and the twine to that open stretch of land, Tiger,' she heard behind her. 'I'll just help Frances with the hamper and I'll be right behind you.'

She heard Jack scurrying off and her heart leapt in the silence that followed. If he dared touch her—

'Frances?'

She whirled around. 'How could you do something like that with Jack about?'

He lifted dark eyebrows. 'You mean, I'm allowed to do it when he isn't?'

She clenched her fists. 'Of course not! I meant . . .'

He gave her a slow smile which completely put her off what she was saying. 'Frances, for heaven's sake, relax. It was just a kiss . . .'

She stared incredulously at him. 'You

haven't even apologised for the first one!'

Suddenly he burst into laughter, warm and deep, which seemed to flow up from the bottom of his cavernous chest under the T-shirt. 'Oh, sweet girl—'

'Don't call me that. And stop laughing at me!' She felt close to tears—but why? she wondered in humiliation. Why was she letting him get to her like this?

His humour mellowed. 'Hey, come on—lighten up. It's a beautiful day, we have every reason to enjoy ourselves and I promise I shan't touch you again if you don't want me to.'

'No, I don't want you to—in front of Jack or at any other time!' She swivelled back to the rugs and scooped up an armful, the corners of her eyes dangerously damp.

He stood very close and she stiffened, sensing his body next to her and all the vibes coming from it. She quailed inside; she trembled. She told herself that she hated him and vowed that if he touched her again she would slap his face—Jack or no Jack.

But he didn't touch her. Instead, he lifted the hamper and said very softly, 'He must have hurt you very deeply, whoever this man was . . . But I'm not him—I'm me, Frances. And please try to see the distinction between us, or what chance have we of ever getting to know one another?'

Then he walked away. Her mouth fell

open. She watched in amazement as the long brown arms lowered the hamper to a patch of green grass, undid the top and shook out the tablecloth. He looked briefly back, brown eyes turned on her. 'It looks delicious,' he called with a smile. 'Back in a moment.'

She could hardly believe it as she walked across to the hamper and sank to her knees.

She was vaguely aware of voices, of Jack yelling with delight and Bruno laughing—that same low, powerful stream of laughter that curled around her senses and made her glance up and stare at him from under her lashes.

How did he know about Greg? Was it just a lucky guess?

Her fingers worked at the preparation but her mind whirled like the Union Jack kite high above them, spinning and diving with its festooned tail of red and blue diamonds jostled in every direction.

Had Greg hurt her so much that she was still punishing men in general? Up till now, she hadn't wanted to admit the pain of their separation, over fourteen months ago. Yet today she'd had to face it And Bruno had forced her to. Was that why she had turned on him so ferociously?

She knew she had overreacted. But she felt so tense when he was around. The temptation to resort to hostility was a kind of self-defence, she supposed, and it was so automatic that she had barely known she was doing it.

135

She laid out Rosa's chicken drumsticks and salad and curled cellophane over the paper plates, her hands working automatically.

Plastic tumblers . . . soft drinks . . . napkins . . . knives and forks . . . plates.

What was it that so disturbed her about Bruno Quillan?

Country fruitcake cut into wedges . . . some of Mrs Dean's cheese and wholemeal biscuits . . .

He was an arrogant, self-centred, self-opinionated—

Salt and pepper . . .

To take her in his arms and kiss her whenever he felt like it . . . Was that what had happened when he'd flashed that smile at Suzie Collins or Meg Fellows? She gave up on the food and sank back on her heels. She was even jealous of Lindsay. She couldn't believe it, but she was.

'Did you see, Fran? Did you see?' Jack fell down beside her breathlessly, eyes a brilliant, happy blue. 'It went higher than it ever had before—almost into outer space!'

She forced herself to smile, and even to say something about the kite's ascent. She realised that whilst one half of her was talking, behaving normally, the other was stunned into numbness, into incredulity at her own fickle, jealous self. The truth was, she didn't hate Bruno Quillan at all. What she hated was the fact that she looked so much like Lindsay—

that this might very well be the reason he was attracted to her!

*   *   *

After the picnic, they drove on a wonderfully clear road to Abbotsbury and sheltered in the cool shadow of St Catherine's Chapel, a beautiful fifteenth-century building with a mysterious stone vault. Jack held her hand as they moved over the cold grey slabs and they read the inscribed names. Then they had afternoon tea in the Purbecks and drove to the coast, where they paddled and fished for crabs. Since none of them had thought to bring beach gear, the rock fishing was laced with a delightful edge of danger lest someone should fall in fully clothed.

Afterwards, Bruno bundled them back into the Range Rover and drove to Lyme Regis and the marine aquarium, where Jack was entranced with the variety of fish and the soft small marine life which he had only ever seen on TV.

Then, thirsty and exhausted; they dozed in the Range Rover as Bruno drove them back to Lulworth and to the castle at dusk.

It was a magical sight. The soft warm breeze blew the musty dust down from the hill to where they stood in the village.

The castle's skeleton blackened as the sun dipped behind it, and the three of them watched in awe as it faded silently into the dusk. Then they sat at the inn at the bottom of the hill on wooden benches and drank glasses of lemonade and ate scampi in the basket.

Frances gazed up at the castle, invisible, closeted in a veil of mist, and as she shivered remembered that she still hadn't given Bruno back his sweater. Jack nudged closer to her on the wooden bench, replete from his meal, his cool arm brushing her skin and his little face aglow with the sunshine of the day.

Automatically her arm slid around him. He gave a great yawn and relaxed into her.

Bruno's dark eyes seemed to be studying them. The evening was so mellow that it didn't seem to matter about the tourists who were still milling slowly around. 'You both look exhausted,' he said gently.

She laughed and nodded. Quite unbelievably, the day had passed as easily as honey sliding over bread; they had laughed and joked and she had forgotten entirely that she had been so angry.

'Better make a move, before we take root.' He smiled as Jack rubbed his eyes.

She looked at the tall shadow opposite her, with the light of the inn blushing out behind him, the deep hollows in his face, the dark eyes staring at her. She noticed everything in that moment and felt the aching attraction—his presence, his powerful body, the dark hairs which grew over his arms, the sinews beneath.

Everything. As though she drank it all at one gulp.

He got up, came around the wooden table and ruffled Jack's head. 'Come along, Tiger, home we go.'

Jack made no protest; he was too tired. They walked slowly across the little square and Frances gave a last glance up to the sleeping castle, aware of Bruno's hand at her waist, his touch lightly guiding her as they went.

Nothing was said in the week that followed about that Sunday. She suspected that Bruno did not wish to broadcast the fact that he had spent the whole day in the company of his district nurse and so, for one reason or another, by mutual consent, it seemed the subject was not to be referred to again.

It suited her well enough. She didn't want to be the cause for gossip or rumour. Look how the stories had circulated about Suzie Collins and Meg Fellows—and heaven alone knew what had happened to precipitate them.

Rosa had phoned her to apologise for falling ill on their picnic day, but had made no mention of asking her over again, and Frances was relieved and yet ridiculously disappointed at the same time.

Early in the week, Frances called at the Clark household.

Sarah had just fed Freddie, who was sound asleep for once.

'How is he?' Frances enquired softly, not

139

wishing to wake the baby.

Freddie's mother shrugged. 'The surgeon performed an operation with a foreign name—I forget it now. But it seems to have cleared up the trouble.'

Frances nodded. 'Ramstedt's operation?'

Sarah looked surprised. 'Do you know of it?'

Frances told her about the twin baby boys in London. She explained carefully that the simple surgery consisted of making an incision in the abdomen to make a cut along the outside of the swollen pylorus, in so doing allowing the passageway inside the pylorus to expand enough to allow the food to pass through. She also explained that the success rate was virtually one hundred per cent.

Sarah sighed. 'Yes . . . I seem to remember the surgeon telling me that too. But I was too . . . too confused to take it all in. I felt . . . felt as though it might have had something to do with me—something I didn't do right, or something that happened when he was in my womb.'

Frances suddenly realised that the young woman was blaming herself for her little boy's problem, and by the way she looked, so pale and tired, she was still very confused. She said gently, 'When Dr Quillan sees Freddie, perhaps it would be a good idea to tell him how you feel. I think he may be able to answer one or two questions that have been worrying you.'

Sarah shook her head firmly, on the brink of tears. 'My husband thinks I need some pills to help me. But I just feel I want to run away from everything.'

Frances was silent for a moment, realising that Sarah was extremely depressed. She would have to get Bruno to see her as quickly as possible. 'Look, try not to worry. Lots of mums feel like this after giving birth. It's quite a natural reaction.'

Sarah wasn't to be comforted. 'But I was over the moon with Joanna. Why am I like this with Freddie?'

It wasn't a question Frances could answer in the space of a few moments, and besides, Sarah herself would be the only one to know the truth. Any advice would have to come from the GP, followed, hopefully, by some kind of treatment.

She left Sarah with an uneasy feeling and hurried back to the surgery, hoping to catch Bruno before he left for his afternoon calls. But he had already gone and she was forced to content herself with writing it in the appointments diary for the next day. She underlined the message in red, marking a large 'Q' beside it for easy reference.

When she went into the surgery the following afternoon, the visit was still not crossed off, and Frances felt the familiar stirrings of unease. Sarah Clark needed immediate attention—hadn't she made it plain enough? Yet the visit was still pending.

Just then Meg Fellows walked out from her room and handed Frances a prescription for one of her housebound patients. 'I know you wanted these antibiotics for your visit to Mrs Jenks tomorrow,' she said, and frowned. 'What's wrong?'

Frances bit her lip. 'I'm sorry. It's just that Sarah Clark—a patient of Dr Quillan's should have been seen this morning—'

'Oh, don't worry,' Meg Fellows broke in quickly. 'Dr. Quillan asked me if I'd see her. Postnatal depression, isn't it?'

Frances was silent for a moment, shocked at Bruno's delegation of Sarah Clark's care. 'Her baby son has just had an op for congenital pyloric stenosis and she's very low.' She shrugged, knowing that the case could not be explained in a matter of minutes. 'I saw her yesterday and she is very, very depressed.'

Meg pushed back her dark hair. She was a handsome woman in her mid-thirties and had a decisive, efficient attitude which Frances imagined she applied as much to her patients as she did to her dinner parties. 'Leave it to me,' she said. 'Anything else?'

Frances shook her head doubtfully and watched her go. Poor Sarah. How could Bruno palm her off like that?

Gill came over from Reception. 'How's it going?'

'Do you really want to know?' Frances muttered grimly.

'Like that, is it?' Gill grinned. 'Some you win, some you lose . . . Oh, by the way, how is Benita? Has she had the baby?'

Frances nodded abstractedly, still preoccupied with the problem of Sarah. 'Yes, a little boy. I had a call last night from her husband to let me know. She's taken the baby to her parents' home in Spain.'

'For a holiday?'

Again Frances nodded, her mind still on Sarah Clark. 'She's staying there for the summer and coming home in September.'

'How does her husband manage?'

Frances thought of the stalwart Derek, whom Benita had earmarked during their training days in the QAs. 'Oh, he's used to the routine of separations. He's a doctor who works for an oil company and is frequently away on rigs.'

'All right for some.' Gill sighed enviously. 'My better half would kick up a real hullabaloo if I left him for even a weekend with the kids!' She hesitated. 'Are you still homesick for London, Frances?'

She was about to say that she was when, much to her own surprise, the thought struck her that she hadn't missed the city at all. Not the hustle and bustle, nor her flat, nor her friends or the old practice.

Crazy, but true, she thought as she said

goodbye to Gill. Driving back to the little flat in Bow Lane, she realised that she had come to regard it as home.

* * *

'Will you calm down and listen?'

'Calm down?' Frances gasped. 'How could you ignore my request in the diary? I made it quite specifically for you, marked with a "Q".'

She pushed Bruno's consulting room door closed. 'I have every right to be annoyed. You promised me you would see Sarah!'

Bruno nodded. 'I know I did. But I had second thoughts. I'm afraid I just couldn't get hold of you to. explain.'

'Explain what? Sarah expected to see you—not Dr Fellows. How can you have ignored her?'

'Frances, I haven't ignored her.'

'You transferred her to someone else—which amounts to the same. She trusted you. She would have confided in you.'

He lifted a hand; 'I'm flattered at your confidence in me—but there are extenuating circumstances here, and if you'll just listen, I'll try to explain them.'

'It's perfectly obvious—'

'No, it isn't!' His voice rose. 'Not unless you're telepathic. Now, for heaven's sake, woman, sit down!'

She dropped into the patient's chair and

144

folded her arms. What excuse was he going to make now? Whatever it was, it had better be a good one!

He sat too. 'That's better. Now . . . if you'll bear with me, I'll tell you what happened.' He took a long breath. 'I'd been toying with the idea of asking Meg to see Sarah—I thought if she improved it might not be necessary, but when I saw your urgent message in the diary I realised I had to make a decision. As it happens, Meg was beside me at the time, looking up her calls, and it seemed appropriate to mention the case.'

'But—'

'And I'm happy to say Meg has met with a measure of success,' Bruno put in swiftly, before Frances could protest 'Sarah explained that she felt guilty for preferring her little girl to Freddie—she explained how sometimes she feels unnaturally cold towards the baby, or regards him with no emotion at all. Her overriding temptation is to run away and escape from the feelings she doesn't understand.'

'She told Dr Fellows that?'

He nodded, dark eyes slightly hooded, long black lashes swooping down to stroke his cheekbones. 'Frances, you are a good nurse, but you tend to think you always know what's best for your patients. Now, I had a special reason for asking Meg to see Sarah Clark.'

Frances said nothing, still bemused as to

145

why Bruno had made the change.

'She's probably the best person to counsel her. Certainly far better than I, and probably better than an outsider.'

'But why?'

He hesitated before looking up at her. 'Meg had the same problem when she gave birth to her second child, Annette. So much so, she had a breakdown and time off work. There was also a third party involved, and her husband left her for a younger woman.' He paused again. 'She had a pretty rough time of it, but finally she came back to work after having therapy. Since then she hasn't looked back. Her experience has brought her a certain reward in so far as this is the type of work she feels she can relate to best.'

Frances was silent. Then she shook her head. 'I had no idea. I wish someone had told me.'

'I would have—if you'd given me time.' He tilted his dark head. 'But this is quite new to all of us—we don't usually swap our patients about unless there is good cause. Sarah will be Meg's first official case. So really you are in from the word go.'

Frances leaned back, sighing. 'I see.' She looked up at him. 'I feel a little foolish now.'

He shrugged. 'You were concerned for your patient. At the same time, I didn't want to be rushed . . . I wanted to see which way the case developed, and I did think the baby's successful return to health might have been the answer. Unfortunately, as you, so astutely diagnosed—far ahead of us mere mortals—it wasn't.'

A knock suddenly interrupted them, and Suzie Collins put her head round the door.

'Oh, sorry!' she apologised flusteredly. 'I didn't realise you had someone with you!'

'It's all right—come in, Suzie.' Bruno shot to his feet. 'Sister Duncan and I have just finished.'

Awkwardly Frances got up and made her way to the door, acknowledging a blushing Suzie before she left.

In the cloakrooms, she splashed cold water on her face. Silly, but she badly needed to compose herself. Bruno had managed to make her feel about two feet tall.

Leaning her head back against the cold wall, she closed her eyes and took a deep breath.

Somewhere along the line, she was going wrong.

But where?

*   *   *

Later, Frances wrote to Serena Rasti, care of her father in Delhi. She had no idea whether, the girl would reply, or even if the letter would reach her safely, so she wrote only the briefest of details. But she made sure that she sent Madjur's love and her hopes that she would reply.

This done, she posted it one evening and walked the short distance from Bow Lane to the Ferryman, where she decided to spoil herself and call in for a cheap bottle of wine to put on ice. The inn was full, thirst having driven many tourists in for a refresher. The off-sales department was situated adjacent to the lounge bar and the garden entrance.

Whilst waiting to be served Frances stared out and admired the smooth green lawn which led down to a brook. Striped umbrellas shielded the tables and birds seemed to fill the air with song.

Her mind turned back to the day she'd been here with Bruno, and the way he had demolished the sandwich. She smiled at the memory.

Her eyes wandered from the garden and back through to the lounge, now filled with chattering tourists, coming to rest on the window seat.

She blinked, and blinked again.

Yes, the woman who sat there was painfully familiar to her, her silver-blonde, hair swept up into a soft chignon. She was deep in conversation with a young man sitting beside her. The kiss between them was brief, unnoticed by most of those around, and Frances realised that she herself would have missed it had she not been studying the corner in which she and Bruno had sat.

Her purchases made, Frances took another swift glance and bit down on her lip. Then she walked slowly outside into the warm summer's evening and wondered whether or not it would be wiser to forget what she had seen— especially since Bruno would think she was merely giving vent to spite, or even retaliating over the Sarah Clark affair.

*   *   *

'I've decided to send Gabriel Bally in for an angiography,' Bruno told Frances the next day. 'He's in with me now and—ah—he'd like to have a word with you.'

'With me?' Frances stared in surprise. 'But you gave me to understand I was the last person he wanted to see!'

'I said the complaint came from his wife, Frances, not Gabriel. Now, are you coming or not?'

She hesitated in the busy office, glancing at the worrying test results he had given her relating to Gabriel Bally. Then she shrugged and followed. She couldn't have incurred Petra Bally's wrath again, for she had studiously avoided the couple! A pity, for it was an interesting case, and she had to agree with Bruno's decision that dealing with the gastrointestinal problem in the home environment without invasive surgery would be better for a man with such high blood
149

pressure and, specifically, the angina which had now been diagnosed through the tests.

Frances walked into the consulting room, bracing herself for trouble all the same.

Gabriel Bally shocked her. If he had looked poorly before, he now looked positively ill. Something in the expression of his eyes, which wasn't physical pain alone, made her gasp. And then, as she sat beside him and he stared at her, she knew that there was more than his illness worrying him. And she was well aware of what it was!

Hesitantly he looked up at her. 'Sister Duncan, I've come to apologise.' He stopped, searching for words. 'Petra has been under a great deal of pressure lately—and her reaction was no fault of yours that day you visited. I understand she made a complaint and I have withdrawn it unconditionally. Will you accept our apology?'

So that was the way of it, Frances thought, with a sad sigh for Gabriel. He was defending her—still. Perhaps he knew—and didn't want to believe it. Perhaps someone in the Ferryman had seen . . . Perhaps he knew long before.

'It's forgotten,' Frances said without rancour. 'How are you feeling?'

He shrugged.

'I'll survive.'

Bruno moved to his seat behind his desk and gave Frances a fleeting glance before he

150

said quietly, 'Mr Bally, I'd like to send you for an angiography. I'm going to start you on a course of drugs that will temporarily increase the blood supply to the heart whilst you are waiting for your appointment.'

Gabriel Bally frowned, his face more anxious than ever. 'What is an angiography?'

Bruno sketched a quick diagram and passed it across the desk. 'I'd like to make sure there is no narrowing or blocking of a coronary artery. There, you see?' Bruno pointed to the map of the heart muscle he had drawn. 'The procedure involves sending a dye into the artery so that it shows up on X-ray. A catheter accesses the artery, usually via the groin, and is threaded upward. It sounds complicated, but it's really quite straightforward. The radiologist is guided by the internal picture on the X-ray screen and pictures are taken *en route* whilst the dye travels along the artery.'

'And can he see then if there's a blockage or something?'

'Well, he'll study the pictures very closely. You'll be in for a few days, I expect.'

The man looked worried. 'I really don't want to spend any more time away from home.' At Bruno's frown Gabriel Bally shrugged again, and leant tiredly back in the chair, finally nodding. 'I suppose so—if you think it's really necessary, Dr Quillan.'

'I want to be absolutely sure we've investigated all angles.'

151

'OK,' agreed his patient dismally. 'I'll wait to hear from you.'

'From the hospital,' Bruno corrected, standing up. 'I'll see where I can get you in the quickest, so you shouldn't have a long wait.'

Frances walked out with Gabriel Bally. 'You're not driving?' she asked as he hesitated at Reception.

'No . . . unfortunately Petra had an appointment this afternoon, so she couldn't chauffeur me.'

Frances gestured to the waiting room. 'Why don't you take the weight off your feet for a moment and I'll call you a taxi?'

He smiled gratefully and sank breathlessly into a chair. Frances phoned for a taxi and when it came walked outside with him, making sure that he was safely on board. She was still deep in thought as she stared into space after the taxi had gone when Bruno appeared beside her, case in hand. She looked up at him, and in the warm sunshine she noticed that his dark eyes had turned a liquid chocolate-brown.

'Not so good,' he said quietly.

Frances nodded. 'His condition is serious, isn't it?'

Bruno heaved his shoulders. 'He may need a coronary bypass.'

It was no surprise to Frances, and she sighed. 'Let's hope he has enough support, at home.' But as she said it she knew that it was wishful thinking, for she could not foresee

Petra Bally giving up her lover for an invalid husband.

Bruno brought her suddenly back down to earth when she was vaguely aware of him speaking.

'Sorry,' she mumbled, 'what did you say?'

His smile was rueful. 'You deserved the apology. Feel better?'

She shrugged. 'Not really. Gabriel Bally never owed me one in the first place.'

His smile widened and he reached out to touch her arm. 'Dinner on Saturday, I insist. My way of making amends for the small percentage of the general public who make a district nurse's life fraught.'

She couldn't help smiling. 'Just the general public?'

His grin spread. 'And the occasional irritating GP?'

'Put like that, I suppose I can hardly refuse.'

He nodded. 'The little Italian bistro in Cerne Carey? We'll arrange the time later.'

And then he was gone, as usual, with the speed of light.

When she turned back and walked into the surgery, wondering why in heaven's name she had agreed so easily, she came face to face with Suzie Collins. She would have liked to bet that the young woman had been watching from the window.

Suddenly she felt rebellious. She experienced a little tremble of excitement

153

down her spine and it felt good. Why shouldn't she? Italian was, after all, her favourite food. And Bruno Quillan ought to feel contrite!

Smiling at Suzie, she drifted breezily past, wondering what she would wear. Mentally reviewing her limited wardrobe, she decided that she would go out after work and lash out on something really special at a little boutique she had noted in town.

CHAPTER SEVEN

'Wow!'

She blushed self-consciously at the frank admiration in the dark eyes. Caught between this and her surprise at seeing him so spruced up in an immaculate dark suit and a cheeky little bow tie—plus a haircut which was a shock in itself—she just managed to find her bag and walk with him to the Range Rover.

The aquamarine silk of the dress she had bought clung to her figure as he lifted her in by her small waist, her slim skirt proving the first barrier to riding in a work-a-day vehicle.

They both laughed at her fragile high heels skimming the metalwork and making a screech, though her own laughter was out of embarrassment and his, she suspected, was to deflect from the enjoyment of seeing the top six inches of silky stockinged leg exposed by the movement.

She pulled the material across quickly, lost her bag, and in the process of trying to catch it almost fell back into his arms

He sat her down. For a second there was a frisson of electricity between them as she took a breath and their eyes met. Then she sat back, blushing again, content to let fate have its way as he pushed the little silver purse into her trembling fingers, arching wry eyebrows. 'All fingers and thumbs tonight, Sister Duncan? Not our usual adept self?'

She couldn't help but smile, and he smiled with her, showing a flash of gorgeous white teeth. Now, she wondered as he jumped in beside her, only last week—even yesterday—she would have taken umbrage at that remark! Tonight she had laughed, able to take the tease.

A fleeting sense of guilt gripped her. Her attitude towards him was changing—though she couldn't fathom out why. Why, over the weeks, had she been so swift to condemn?

Then, with an even deeper sense of guilt, she remembered the other Bruno Quillan, whom she had tried to deliberately block from her mind—the one who wore silly shirts and sunglasses and who clowned around in a pale blue swimming pool on a beautiful summer's day.

In Giovanni's, the mood was low-key and candlelit. The atmosphere was soothed by

Mediterranean music and the scent of exotic cooking.

At the table they ordered the meal, though Frances could not have said what it was, because time stood still as she sat there. She felt absorbed by those deep brown eyes, which seemed to magnetise all of her attention. He made her laugh—and laugh. The butts of his humour were cases from his training days and anecdotes from his time abroad as a student. A little nonsense was of Rosa and Jack and Christina, his sister-in-law. Then there were a few anecdotes of his brother and the family abroad.

All so easily related, until she realised that they had finished every last crumb of the succulent tagliatelle, beautiful hot bread and sweet fruits which had had a soft Italian flavour of wine and cream.

Finally he leant back. She guessed what he was about to do. He whipped off the bow tie and undid the button beneath, closing his heavy-lidded eyes in pure pleasure. 'Ah . . . whoever thought up the idea of these tortuous pieces of attire has a lot to answer for!'

She laughed, thinking how sexy he looked sitting there. The dark jacket fell open across a white shirt, and she vaguely wondered if Rosa had ironed the shirt for him. Her eyes were swift to notice the broad chest beneath, the tease of curling blackness thrusting upward into the tanned well of his throat. And all that lovely dark hair, tamed into a fashionable collar-length cut flicked back from his face. Oddly, the thought of this brought back a sudden reminder.

'Your sweater!' she gasped, her hand going to her mouth.

'I wondered when I would ever see it again!'

She looked dismayed. 'It's still in the car. I'd forgotten—'

He leaned forward and took her hand. 'I'm only teasing. Keep it—for another rainy day.'

The sensation of his fingers on hers made her catch her breath, and she was quite unprepared for what he said next.

'Frances,' he murmured softly, 'tell me who he was.'

Astonished, she gazed at him, with her long straight hair in a fawn veil over her shoulders, resting softly on the aquamarine silk straps, and the softness and cool beauty of her complexion making her look like delicate porcelain in the subdued light.

'There was someone, wasn't there?'

'I don't think—'

'Are you still in love with him?'

She licked her dry top lip, overly conscious of her hectic pulse-rate and the firm grasp of his hand. 'No,' she said, and swallowed. 'It's over.'

'Just because it's over doesn't mean to say you're not still in love with him.'

She looked into the warm brown eyes. 'Greg was in the Army,' she told him, the words coming out stiffly. 'I was training with the QAs when we met, and he was with a special unit I didn't really think much about the implications then—in fact, I suppose it all seemed rather glamorous at first. Then, six months later, he was almost killed in a Belfast explosion.' She took a breath. It was the first time she had discussed Greg with anyone. 'I tried to tell myself I wasn't worried—that I wasn't living on a knife-edge . . . waiting for the news over the television . . . or a phone call . . .'

'But you were?'

She nodded slowly. 'I'd lived my childhood in an army environment; I could cope with that. I understood the pressures, accepted there would be long separations. I knew the way service families always travelled out of suitcases, never knowing which posting was next. But I began to notice that Greg lived off the adrenalin of his work, the danger. That was what I couldn't cope with.'

'Wasn't there another alternative?'

She looked at him strangely. 'A change of regiment, you mean?' She shook her head. 'When it came to the crunch, Greg chose the Gulf—special missions.'

'I'm sorry, Frances.'

The pain she had been waiting for did not come. Instead, she looked into his eyes, and they were moving over her. He lifted her hand

and kissed it. 'Your Greg was a foolish fellow.'

She was aware that her hand burned where his lips had touched. 'So . . . now you've prised my seriously boring past out of me, what about you?' she asked quickly, to change emphasis.

He grinned. 'Haven't I spent all evening quoting you my little anecdotes, or haven't you been listening?'

'Oh, yes, I've been listening. More to what you haven't said than what you have.'

He lowered her hand and gently laid it on the table, staring up at her. The smile was still on his lips, but she could read those dark, brooding eyes by now. She saw the pain. It was all there—deeply hidden, but there all the same. 'I'm sorry. I shouldn't have asked.' She sighed, wishing that she hadn't. 'At least Greg is alive—you had no choice in the matter when Lindsay died.'

He lifted his face. 'That's not strictly true, I'm afraid.'

She frowned, waiting, wondering if he would go on. He hesitated, forming the words slowly as he spoke. 'Lindsay and I met when we were students, but she dropped out—I should have seen how restless she was then, and tried to do, something about it. But she insisted on leaving medical school—and, foolishly, I encouraged her. When I qualified, we married. I thought she might settle, but . . . as restless as ever, she opened a small interior design business. For, a while it contented her.'

159

Frances frowned. 'Then surely she was happy?'

'I'm afraid not. I suppose I just didn't measure up to what she expected.' He looked down, absently playing with a fork. 'I realised quite early on our relationship was going wrong, and I tried to pull it together the best I could. I was forced to ignore her indiscretions—I just prayed they wouldn't become common knowledge.' He looked up, regarding her steadily . . . 'I was determined we should stay together for Jack's sake.'

'Oh, Bruno . . . I had no idea.'

He lifted dark brows. 'I never really thought she would leave—take Jack—that's what was so strange, so shattering. But then . . . when I'd had time to adjust, I realised I didn't want her back—it would have only been for Jack's sake.'

'And Jack?' she asked softly. 'Does he remember any of it?'

'Not as far, as I can tell. He was only four when she died. The car Lindsay was driving went off the road. They think she may have fallen asleep at the wheel. She was killed outright, but her boyfriend survived.' His voice had sunk to a gruff whisper.

'I'm sorry—truly.' She wanted to reach out and comfort him. 'But at least Jack wasn't in the car.'

He looked down at the table again, absorbed in the memory. 'Rosa was babysitting him, thank God. Lindsay had no qualms about

160

dropping him off when she felt like it. Poor Rosa. She took the brunt of everything—she had to cope with me and Jack and her own grief. She's been a tower of strength.'

Frances nodded. 'Yes, she's a wonderful lady.'

The coffee came and they drank quietly. He sat back and looked at her for a long time. 'If Rosa hadn't occupied the maternal role in Jack's life,' he said at last, so softly that she could barely hear him, 'it would have been devastating for him. She knew . . .' He hesitated, looking at her from under his dark lashes. 'She knew that I could not risk him being hurt again.'

For the first time she realised just how much Jack's happiness meant to him—possibly at the cost of his own. She wanted to tell him that she intended in no way to threaten that happiness, for she loved the boy dearly. She was about to speak when he sat forward, resting his elbows on the table.

'There's something else I've been meaning to say,' he said, clearing his throat and making a successful attempt to change the subject. 'Simply that I'm sorry.'

She lifted soft brows. 'What on earth for?'

'For such a terrible start.

She smiled, then drew a breath. 'It was my fault too. I felt resentful because there was no communication between us in that first week. I thought you'd taken an on the spot dislike to me.'

'You had a right to feel resentful,' he agreed, lifting his dark eyes. 'I can only say I felt in some way threatened myself.'

His words swept away any residue of resentment she still felt and she smiled, her blue eyes aglow with warmth. 'Perhaps we were both too quick to make assumptions?'

He sighed. 'How could any man take a dislike to such a lovely creature? No . . . no . . . it wasn't that at all.'

Had not the waiter arrived and asked if there was anything else they would like and the course of conversation been diverted, Frances felt sure that he would have said more—much more. She had the curious feeling that he wanted to tell her something, and yet the moment passed.

They drove home in silence. Now there was something oddly distinctive in the air. A kind of electrical charge. As though two components had been melded together and the outcome was an invisible, very powerful force of energy. It seemed to lie between them, simmering. Her body was alert to it, her senses in overdrive.

She shivered—and not with the sultry night air.

He didn't say a word on the journey home—and what was there to say? she asked herself. Small talk seemed somehow irreverent after what she had learned of Lindsay.

He drove her straight back to the flat. She was disappointed, but not surprised. She didn't want the evening to end, but she supposed it must. Her heart beat fast as they neared Bow Lane. Should she ask him in for coffee?

The Range Rover glided to a halt.

Bow Lane was shrouded in darkness, with a few streetlights spreading a hazy glow over the narrow road. He switched off the engine and took her hand. 'You're trembling?'

She nodded, staring into the shadows of his face. 'Yes, I'm afraid I am. Ridiculous, isn't it?'

'Because of me?'

She shook her head, swallowing. 'No . . .' He said, very softly, 'You feel it too, don't you?'

'Yes,' she managed to stammer.

'Look, I have to tell you this . . .' He sighed deeply before she could speak, and his fingers tightened on her hand. 'Because I think it's important you know . . .'

Don't say it! she cried silently. Don't spoil the magic of the night. He was going to tell her about his casual flings with Suzie and Meg—and that after Lindsay, he had decided not to become seriously involved again.

'I've been wondering how to tell you . . . It seems a pathetic thing to say . . . I don't know how . . .'

Oh, please no, she prayed, tears already stinging behind her lids. What kind of mistake have I made? She'd been hurt by Greg and yet she still hadn't learnt her lesson. All she had done was lay herself open to yet more heartache.

'I know,' she said haltingly, her hand going to the door. 'Rather, I understand,' she corrected herself in a clipped, brisk tone, wanting only to be able to leave the vehicle with the last vestiges of her pride intact. 'And I think perhaps we've come to the point where we should say goodnight and . . . ah . . . it's been a lovely evening.' She grabbed the handle flusteredly and pushed open the door. 'Thank you.'

'Frances, wait—'

She swung her legs down and began to run across the cobbled lane. At the front porch, she thrust her key in the lock, slammed the door behind her and fled upstairs.

In the small front room she stood quite still, shaking.

It was some time before she heard the RangeRover start up. She listened to its growl as it turned in the street below and the powerful headlights reflected across the ceiling, finally diminishing and leaving the room in darkness.

Still in darkness, she sank down onto the sofa, buried her head in her hands and let the tears fall.

*　　　*　　　*

It was a miserable fortnight, drifting into a wet

164

and chilly July.

Bruno was polite to her, but distanced, and she responded similarly.

The most unexpected of things happened when one bleak day she called at the Groves' house and discovered Jack there also. Gwen nodded to the two boys from the kitchen window as Frances walked in. They were dressed in anoraks and Carl was charging around the lawn displaying his rugby technique, grasping an oval ball in his hands and kicking it high over a goalpost that had been erected at the bottom of the vast garden.

'We asked Bruno if Jack would like to spend time with us and keep Carl company in the holidays,' Gwen explained. 'But apparently he's off to a relative soon, and he can only stay the day.'

Frances remembered that Jack was due to go to Christina, Bruno's sister-in-law, and watched with great sympathy as the tiny little figure dragged around the wet garden after Carl, who was thumping the ball here and there for all he was worth.

'Lad's got a good style,' Richard Grove said as the three of them stood looking out into the damp afternoon. 'Harrington Hall certainly toughens 'em up.'

'Poor little Jack,' Gwen said, echoing Frances's thoughts. 'He finds it hard to keep up.'

'Then again—' Frances found herself

defending him '—all children are different. Jack is a natural with technology. He's very skilled on his computer.'

'Oh, Carl can't be doing with sitting in front of a machine,' Richard Grove dismissed. 'He's the outdoor type. Got a big career ahead of him in sport.'

Frances turned away from the window and gestured towards the front room. 'Shall we take a look at the hand, Mr Grove?'

With difficulty she kept her attention on what she was doing. The wound had lost the redness and seemed to have healed. The finger was flexible without giving any pain, and the antibiotics seemed to have effected a cure. Whilst her patient extolled the virtues of Harrington Hall and his hopes for his son to become a professional sportsman Frances cleaned the long thin scar with antiseptic.

'I think we can leave the dressing off.' She was forced to interrupt as the diatribe seemed to be endless. 'You're in luck. The wound has healed remarkably well after the infection.'

'All in the mind,' the big man informed her boastfully. 'I've had that dressing off one or two times in the past week and managed to do a bit of work without any problem.'

'I wouldn't have recommended that,' Frances remarked severely. 'If you had picked up some dirt—'

'Don't you start nagging at me too,' he laughed. 'Had enough from the wife.'

166

Frances glanced at Gwen Grove, who commented drily that she had washed her hands of trying to keep her husband in line.

At that moment the boys rushed in, and Jack stopped in his tracks. 'Fran!' he exclaimed, plainly delighted.

'Hi, Jack.' She gave him a warm smile, restraining herself from too fond an overture, sensitive to the curious glances of Gwen and Richard.

Carl pushed past and lumped his dirty rugby shoes onto the table. His father picked them up and, with a sigh removed them to the kitchen—to Frances's consternation, using his vulnerable hand. Hesitating, she looked once more at Gwen, who simply lifted her brows.

'Well, I must be going,' Frances said, and began to pack her case, realising that whatever she said to Richard Grove went in one ear and out the other.

'Can I come with you?' Jack stood beside her, his blue eyes staring up like huge great blue moons.

Frances hesitated. After the scene with his father she had promised herself to disengage gently. 'Oh, Jack, I'm sure Mrs Grove has supper prepared—'

'We've eaten already,' Jack interrupted, his gaze imploring. 'And Mrs Grove has to drive me home. It will save you the trouble, won't it, Mrs Grove?'

The older woman laughed. 'Well, driving

you home is no trouble, Jack, but if Sister Duncan doesn't mind . . .'

Frances shrugged. 'I don't mind, but . . .' She sought for an excuse without hurting the boy. 'What about your grandmother? She may not be at home.'

'Oh, Grandma is!' Jack beamed at her. 'She said she was spring cleaning today.'

Frances glanced at Gwen hopelessly, but Gwen merely laughed again. 'Must be something I put in the trifle!' she joked, and bustled about collecting coats and wellies and pushing the boys into the cloakroom to wash.

Finally, in the hallway, Gwen smiled. 'Bruno's boy obviously likes you a lot,' she prompted, frowning curiously. 'You seem very close.'

'He's a nice lad,' Frances deliberately understated. She knew that Gwen was prodding and she certainly wasn't going to enlarge.

She was relieved to see Jack reappear, and made a last entreaty regarding her patient. 'Do try to impress on your husband that he must be careful with his hand,' she advised briskly.

'Thanks for the nice day, Mrs Grove!' Jack was out of the door and halfway up the drive.

Frances shrugged and smiled apologetically, somewhat embarrassed. It was evident that Jack couldn't wait to get clear of the house!

'Have you got any of those chocolate mousses at your flat, Fran?' he asked as they

168

drove off, and Frances stared open-mouthed at him.

'Jack! I thought you wanted to go home?'

He chuckled. 'Not really. Can we go to your flat?'

She frowned in concern at the tiny figure on her passenger seat. 'Weren't you enjoying yourself at the Groves'?'

He shrugged. 'It was OK, but they go on and on about Harrington Hall all the time.'

She looked at him in concern. 'And you don't want to talk about your new school?'

He shook his head. 'Not much.'

Frances sadly turned her attention back to the road. 'I don't think your grandmother would want me whisking you off somewhere,' she resisted. 'What would happen if she phoned Mrs Grove only to discover you were with me?'

Jack giggled. 'Oh, she never minds if I'm with you. She likes you a lot. I could ring her from your flat, couldn't I?'

Frances realised with a sigh that she had lost the battle!

*   *   *

Jack duly telephoned and Frances had a quick word with Rosa, who said that she wasn't at all surprised her grandson had wriggled out of staying at the Groves', for he was never inclined to go there and had put up enough

169

obstacles first thing this morning, when Gwen had rung.

There were no chocolate mousses in the freezer, but she resurrected a packet of Neapolitan ice cream from under a packet of brussels sprouts and they ate more or less the whole lot between them.

'May we play Monopoly?' Jack asked as they cleared away the dishes.

'I don't think we've time. What about Scrabble?'

'Ace!' He dashed to the cupboard in which he knew Frances kept the games, her own from childhood, eagerly drawing out all the different boxes.

Watching him throughout the evening, she thought what a bright, perceptive and articulate child he was when in an atmosphere in which he could relax. He noticed everything, played with enthusiasm, and his spelling was remarkably good. At the end of the game they totalled the score and it was a close thing, with her winning by a small margin. She had deliberately kept her choice of words simple at first, but it wasn't long before her opponent had had her working hard to make her rack her brains.

Driving him home later, she dreaded seeing Bruno, thinking he might take it that she had captured Jack deliberately. She was just wondering how to explain what had happened when Jack spoke.

'Do you know I'm going to board at Harrington Hall in September?' he asked quietly.

She nodded. 'Your father told me.'

There was a long silence and she glanced at him, taking her eyes from the road for a moment.

'Dad says it's a good school,' he said dully—and to Frances's mind loyally.

'I'm sure it is.'

'I 'spect I'll get used to it'

Frances cast her eyes back to the road. 'I'm sure you will.'

Her heart tightened. She had adapted to being away from her parents, but then she had been the type of child who could cope with the environment of boarding-school. There had been others friends of hers, quieter, sensitive children—who had never adapted. She wondered if Jack had the resources to cope, and she wondered, most of all, why Bruno had decided on such a step.

At the house, she helped Jack out with his things and they walked to the front door. Bruno opened it before they arrived and her heart seemed to leap right out of her body at the sight of him.

He ruffled Jack's hair. 'Hi, Tiger.'

Jack spent the next five minutes in telling his father about the evening he'd spent at Bow Lane, with not a mention of the Groves'. Then he bounded off to find his grandmother who,

171

Bruno said, was in her own part of the house.

When Jack had gone Bruno sought her eyes. 'It was kind of you to bring him home.'

She gazed up into his dark stare, aware that he had never looked more attractive. A subtle shadow edged his jaw and she knew that if she lifted her fingers it would be rough and hard to the touch, and if she drew her hand down over the sweatshirt-clad torso it would feel smooth and muscled.

Wasn't it ridiculous? She had made it clear that she wasn't interested, and here she was . . .

Her body trembled. She longed to be in his arms. She wanted him so much!

As if in unspoken reply, he drew her into his arms and, muttering an oath, brought his mouth down hard on hers, pushing his tongue between her teeth so that she opened her mouth and let him in on a hungry, wanton gasp of desire.

'I've missed you, my darling,' he whispered, kissing her again and again with tiny butterfly kisses, his body hard against her.

She slid her arms around his neck and sighed so deeply that she knew the breath had come from her soul. 'And I've missed you,' she murmured achingly, wondering if he realised, just how much she meant it.

CHAPTER EIGHT

It was a hungry, passionate kiss of deep longing.

Right there on the doorstep, with the soft night air blowing in, the radio playing from somewhere in the house and her heart sounding like a drum in her ears. His fingers gripped her arms tightly as he pressed her to him, the pressure of the kiss telling her that whatever she did he meant to kiss her—that this was no mistake, no casual embrace.

She gasped, straining for breath, pushing her hands against his chest.

He wouldn't let her go. 'Frances, I've got to see you.'

She was terrified that Jack might reappear. 'Someone might come—'

'Then say you'll see me.'

Aware that she had no choice in the matter, she sighed. 'All right, but let me go . . . please.'

Slowly he set her free. 'Tomorrow?'

She nodded, feeling shaken

'Can I come to your place . . . after surgery?' She hesitated. 'I don't think so—'

'Frances, I have to see you—alone.'

Just then Jack came crashing back through the door of the annexe, Rosa following him, and in desperation Frances sent a nod of agreement towards Bruno. However she

173

managed to sound coherent, she didn't know, but she managed—just—saying her goodbyes and then driving home in a daze, wondering what kind of fool she was to allow him to come to the flat.

All night she worried about it, and in the morning she stared in the mirror and saw two great dark rings beneath her eyes. In contrast, the weather was glorious. The day revealed a sky of white fluffy clouds, the overnight rain having enhanced the greens and golds of the gardens.

On arriving at the practice, the first person she collided with was Suzie Collins.

It was a sharp reminder that she knew little of Bruno's past, and then, to compound her doubts, Meg Fellows came into the office and seemed quite chatty, talking about Sarah Clark, with whom she'd begun counselling sessions.

When Frances left on her calls, she was aware that she had barely listened to what Meg had said, other than understanding the gist of it, which was that, happily, Sarah was responding. This was good news, but even so her mind had wandered.

She had agreed to Bruno coming to the flat, for heaven's sake! He was obviously content not to nurture permanent relationships after Lindsay—he'd made no pretence of that. And who could blame him after the way he and Jack had suffered? Did that mean she had to accept the fact that she was embarking on an affair which she knew had no resolution, no possibility of ever maturing? Just how high a price was she prepared to pay to satisfy her need of him?

The day dragged its feet, as well she'd known it would. Two diabetic ladies with their sugar levels to be checked for Nigel, a catheter to be changed on an elderly gentleman for Tristan, and several post-op cases to be seen, to make assessment of their present mobility. The medical profile on each had to be updated, which took longer than anticipated, and then she had to work slowly with a new psychiatric patient who needed special care services at home.

She was relieved, at least, not to have bumped into Bruno. The surgery was chaotic and she just managed to slip away at five without being noticed, dashed to the Delectable Delly in Cerne Carey and bought a few things, then hurried home to shower.

Afterwards, wrapped in a thick, fluffy towel, she took a deep breath and paused by the open window overlooking the garden, breathing in the crystal-clear fresh air, wondering if there was time to ring him and cancel.

It was going to be a beautiful evening weatherwise.

All trace of cloud had disappeared and a glorious sun still shone in the sky. She was just about to pick up the phone when the doorbell went. She stood where she was, her heart pounding. Then slowly she walked to the intercom.

'It's me,' announced the deep voice. 'May I come up?'

He was miles early! She wasn't even dressed yet! Hesitantly she pressed the button which allowed him entry, then ran to the bedroom.

The place looked like a tip!

Rejecting her cast-offs for a clean white robe, she drew it tightly around her and fastened the belt with shaky fingers. She glanced in the mirror. Her hair! She thrust her fingers through its soaking wet thickness and promptly gave up as footsteps were audible on the stairs.

'Sorry I'm early,' he apologised, standing in the lounge as she hurried through, from the bedroom. He was so tall in the tiny room! Dressed in formal blue shirt, navy tie and dark trousers, she realised that he must have come straight from the surgery.

'I wasn't expecting you yet—w-would you like some coffee?'

'I don't want anything.' His voice was so husky it sent a sharp crack of adrenalin into her bloodstream. 'All I want is you.'

He came towards her and enveloped her in his arms, pressing her wet head against his chest. 'Oh, Frances, you don't know how much I need you, but after that night—'

She reached up. 'Bruno . . . I said I

understood.'

'But you don't,' he contradicted her firmly 'You see, I wanted to try to explain how I felt when I first saw you—'

'Because I'm like Lindsay, you mean?'

He stared at her, his jaw dropping. 'You know?'

She nodded. 'Gill told me. Oh, she wasn't gossiping. I think it came out before she'd had time to think.'

'I suppose it was bound to. I'm sorry it had to be that way.' He held her face between his hands. 'I even put away the photos at home. Bloody stupid, of course, but I cared about hurting you. Instinctively I knew that discovering you were like Lindsay might make you reluctant to . . .'

'To have an affair with you?'

He closed his eyes and drew her head onto his chest. 'Oh, Frances, I was desperate when Lindsay took Jack away, and I swore I would never expose either of us to that kind of pain again.' He took a deep breath, seeming to be trying to find the right words without hurting. 'It was just so shattering seeing you standing there that first day. Then, when you turned around, I saw you were so different. Your features were softer and your mouth sweet, your eyes, were warm and gentle—they all held quite a different expression from my wife's . . . but for that moment . . . for one single moment . . .'

'You thought I was her?' she repeated dully.

He nodded, moistening his lips with his tongue. 'As time went by, of course, I realised you, were nothing like her—at least, you bore a resemblance—she was fair and blue-eyed like you, and she wore her hair long—but in character you're both so different . . . two entirely different people.'

She swallowed. 'Yes, I had a suspicion. I thought with Jack's looks and you so very dark . . .'

'He takes after her—physically, yes.'

'But why has he never said anything? He never mentions her, rarely talks about the past.'

'I suppose because he was so young when she died. His memories are fractured. I have to be thankful he remembers so little pain.'

'Poor Jack.' She pushed herself away, her brow pleated in concern. 'Don't you know I could never hurt him? He means so much to me. Which is why I've been trying to . . . to give him space . . .'

'I know.' He smiled. 'I know.'

Her brain seemed so confused. She didn't know whether she was hurt or relieved, or whether she wanted to laugh or cry.

'Frances?' His voice reverberated deeply in her ear as she laid her head on his chest. Her body ached for him—she wanted him, she needed him. But she wondered who he held in his arms.

'Frances, I need you. God help me, I only know I need you now.'

She closed her eyes. 'And I need you too,' she whispered on a sigh as he brought her chin up to his mouth and kissed her with a passion that obliterated every thought from her mind except the need she felt. The torment of doubt was washed temporarily away as in those few moments his tongue teased open her teeth and made a slow, sensual, conquering of her mouth, as his hands pushed against the fabric of her robe, sliding over her warm, naked skin to cup the full swell of her breasts.

She sighed with pleasure, the burning effect of his touch making all her worries evaporate into thin air as she sank helplessly with him to the sofa, no longer caring what mattered or what didn't.

Cool fingers stroked her, her white robe falling open as she lay there, exposed to his hungry gaze. 'You are so beautiful, my darling girl. I want to make love to you . . . I don't want to hurt you.'

Somehow the words which should have reassured her brought her back sharply into focus—for, if she was beautiful, was she beautiful as in Lindsay's image?

When he kissed her, was he thinking of Lindsay?

Had it been the truth when he'd told her that he had not wanted Lindsay back, that although he had been devastated when she'd left him, he would have only tried again for Jack's sake?

She held his head as he nestled into her breast, kissing the rosy bud which sprang to attention between his lips.

'Do you want me to stop?' His voice was rough, but strangely gentle. He eased himself up and looked at her with questioning brown eyes, a deep flush of need burning his cheeks.

'I . . . I'm not sure.' She gazed at him helplessly.

Slowly he lifted himself from her, his tie askew, the buttons of his shirt undone, revealing a wealth of dark, hair-strewn muscle. She ached to pull him back to her. But his hands folded the white robe over her breasts. He tied her belt and then drew her up and into his arms, and they sat there quietly.

'Then I'll wait, until you are,' he said at last 'But if I stay . . .' He kissed her, holding her head between his hands. 'Don't come down. I'll see myself out.'

She looked up into the brown, beautiful eyes. 'Bruno?' she murmured softly. 'May I ask you something?'

He smoothed the damp hair from her face. 'What is it?'

She took a breath. 'Are you involved with anyone else?'

His dark eyes held her for a few moments and then he shook his head. 'No. There's been no one since Lindsay. Not until the moment

180

I walked into the house and saw you standing with Jack, with hair as damp and as lovely as it is now.'

Was he telling her the truth?

He kissed her again, deeply and hungrily, as if to convince her. A minute or two more and she wouldn't have had the strength to let him go. But he was suddenly hauling himself up and away, hurrying down the stairs.

She heard the outer, door close quietly after him with a soft whoosh. Then she waited for the Range Rover to start up, and as the noise of the engine faded into the distance she returned to stare from the window, folding her arms across her aching breasts and shivering ...

*　　　*　　　*

Something happened during the following week to confirm what Bruno had told her and to make her realise that she had been a fool to listen to surgery gossip, however well-meaning Gill might have meant to be.

Cynthia Vail took a turn for the worse and her home help called for a doctor. Nigel Drew was on call and made a visit, finally asking Frances to see what she could do in the way of persuading the elderly lady to bathe, since Cynthia flatly refused to see a community nurse.

Cynthia's almshouse was being painted

by the local borough, and as Frances called there seemed to be a lot going on that would normally have interested the pensioner. There was, however, a scowl on her face as she let Frances in.

'Had a terrible virus for two weeks,' Cynthia complained bitterly. 'And here I was, almost starving to death.' Cynthia led the way into her small lounge, a thick dressing gown muffled up to her chin.

'But I thought you had a home care assistant?'

Cynthia looked sheepish. 'Didn't get on with her at all. Prefer my Suzie to run my errands. Only she couldn't make it last week.'

'Suzie?'

'You know—works at your place. She's my niece.'

Suddenly it clicked. Suzie Collins. And that was how Cynthia gleaned her news! 'Yes, I know Suzie,' Frances said quietly, realising that Cynthia was waiting for her to show surprise. 'Well, now, how about a bath, Mrs Vail? Is the water hot?'

It took a great deal of persuading to get Cynthia into a bath. Frances brought in a special bath-seat from the car which she had decided to request from stores. This trick worked. It appealed to Cynthia, who had previously sworn that no one would ever 'do' for her. The cream which Frances had also thought to bring for any bedsores harboured by a furtive Cynthia also came in handy, and gave great relief to a pair of very sore buttocks. Doubtless Nigel Drew had laboured long and hard to get Cynthia to try and redress the balance of nature.

When Cynthia was dry and dressed in fresh, clean clothing, Frances whipped off her plastic apron and gloves and rolled them into a neat ball for disposal. Cynthia tottered around the kitchen making tea, chattering away.

As no fresh assessment of Cynthia had been done lately, Frances sat herself at the table and began on updating the careplan. She waded through the most important issues with Cynthia, who for once was acquiescent. They managed to cover day and night care, social services and meals on wheels and had a fairly comprehensive look at what she was able to do independently, achieving most of the goals re-established for her.

'They shan't be burying me just yet, then!' Cynthia's tone was wry as they drank the tea. 'Now, how's that doctor that my niece is always going on about—the one with the little boy?'

'Dr Quillan's fine, if that's who you mean,' Frances said briskly, realising that it was time to beat a retreat, and began to pack away her case.

'Oh, yes. That's who I mean, all right. Suzie tells me all the latest. She's a good girl, but she was in with a layabout boyfriend. He spent all their money and sat at home all day doing nothing Mind you, money's always been my Suzie's problem—or maybe the lack of it. That's why I give her a good few pounds when she runs errands for me.'

Frances smiled to herself as she cleared the table. 'Oh, well, I'm sure Suzie knows how to cope.'

Cynthia cackled. 'Well, actually, she doesn't. If it hadn't been for that doctor giving her a good talking to, she would have been in a real pickle. He allowed her an advance on her wages to pay her debts, and finally she got rid of the gormless fool who had been sponging off her. But if it hadn't been for the fact she talked her problems over with Dr Quillan, I dread to think what state she'd have ended up in. She would probably be behind bars by now.'

Frances stood quite still, staring at the tea things. Mechanically, she picked them up, took them to the kitchen and washed them. So that was what it had all been about! Gill and the other girls had jumped to the wrong conclusion—and so had she, for that matter.

As though a weight had been taken off her shoulders, Frances drove back home to Bow Lane. When she arrived there, the phone was ringing.

She picked it up and heard Jack's voice. 'Fran? I'm going to Aunt Christina's next Sunday for two weeks. Can you come over so I can say goodbye?'

'Well, I'm—'

'Oh, please, Fran. Come on Saturday for a swim, and then Grandma says we can have another picnic. Dad can't come this time,' he added, echoing her thoughts. 'I asked him, but he's on call after emergency surgery.'

Was Bruno saying that for her sake? Ever since that evening at the flat over a week ago, he'd been distant—not in an unfriendly fashion, but all the same he'd made it clear that he wasn't going to railroad her, and for that she was grateful. She wanted to be absolutely sure of her feelings . . . and of his.

'All right, Jack,' she agreed weakly. 'What time?'

They made it ten o'clock and he rang off She was growing fonder of the boy and she couldn't stop herself! But the last thing she wanted was to appear as if she was trying to step into his mother's shoes.

Was that what Bruno was looking for? Did she fit the bill as a clone of Lindsay as both mother and wife? The thought made her shudder again. It was as though she had no real identity of her own, as if she needed to pinch herself to make sure she really was Frances Duncan. Perhaps she only warmed Bruno's heart—but hadn't captured it. After all, no one ever loved a fake as much as they loved an original.

*   *   *

On Saturday, when they crowded into the Clio, it was overcast and muggy.

Taking a raincheck on the swim, since the mysterious sky looked so threatening, they headed for Gorley Wood, a local beauty spot with picturesque travellers' huts and wooden picnic benches.

There were one or two families already there, with children playing in the brook under the trees, and Rosa and Frances had time to sit and talk whilst Jack made friends with the other boys, splashing about in the water.

'Not a wheeze in sight,' Rosa marvelled as she sampled a lemon meringue pie from Mrs Dean's. 'Mmm, scrumptious.'

'When was his last attack?' Frances tested a piece for herself

'Oh—way back. When I was in the Lakes with my friend, I think.' She nodded thoughtfully. 'Yes, that awful week when you found him in Cerne Carey.'

'Has he ever told you the reason why he skipped school?'

Rosa put down her spoon and sighed. 'No, but, it doesn't take much working out. I think he must have overheard Bruno and I discussing Harrington Hall the night before. I had the feeling he hadn't gone to bed—his light was still on. Bruno thought he was in his computer room, but I wouldn't be surprised if he'd been listening on the landing.'

'Oh dear, Rosa,' Frances groaned and

186

stared into space. 'He really is dreading Harrington Hall, isn't he?'

'Why don't you talk to Bruno about it?' Rosa put in carefully, touching her arm. 'He would listen to you. I only seem to make matters worse.'

'Well, I've tried a little.' She shrugged. 'But I don't really have the right to interfere.'

Rosa lifted her eyes and smiled. 'He thinks a great deal of you. I'm sure he would consider anything you said very seriously.'

Frances was quiet for a moment, and then Rosa laid a hand over hers.

'You're in love with him, aren't you, my dear?'

Her immediate reaction was to deny it, but it all seemed so silly. Her feelings must be written all over her by now—and yet she was still resisting, even to Rosa, who had, perhaps, guessed all along.

'Yes . . . yes, I think I am,' she said at last, on a deep sigh. 'Am I being a fool, do you think?' Her heart plummeted as Rosa's face changed. After all, Lindsay had been Rosa's daughter!

'I think, Frances, there is something you should know first. Something we must talk about—'

Just then Jack came running over, bringing another boy with him, and they chattered away excitedly. For a fleeting moment Rosa caught Frances's eye as she passed a slice of the pie

187

over to each boy. She said softly, 'Don't worry, we'll talk later!'

Though 'later' was never to come. The day passed so swiftly that their conversation was forgotten until Frances found herself unloading the remnants of the picnic back at the house. It slipped out of her mind again as Jack hugged her and said goodbye, promising to send a postcard from Brighton.

*   *   *

On the Monday after Jack had gone on holiday, Bruno came quietly into the office and closed the door behind him. She looked up from where she was sitting, going over her cases for the day.

'Busy?' He came to stand beside her.

Every muscle in her body tensed. 'No, not really.' She was suddenly all fingers and thumbs, his presence unsettling her as it always seemed to, his dark eyes making a shiver of excitement run down her spine. 'Did Jack get off all right?'

He nodded. 'Fine, thanks. He enjoyed the picnic—thanks for taking them. Quite honestly I think he'd have been happy enough to stay at home.' He looked at her for a long while and then perched on the edge of the desk. 'Frances, have you given us any thought?'

Somehow she had known he was going to ask her that. She nodded slowly. 'Yes, yes . . . I

188

have.'

'And?'

'I agree . . . we should talk.'

'Then see me tonight. I'm not on call. We could have dinner—'

'Better still,' she suggested softly, lifting her blue eyes, 'let me cook supper at the flat.'

Sooner or later she would give in. She was too weak, she loved him too much to resist any more—despite her misgivings. She was not letting herself think of why he wanted her, only that he did want her

Her heart raced as he leant across and bent down to brush her lips. 'You're sure?' he asked softly, the touch of his mouth so sensitive on her lips that she trembled.

'I'm sure.'

And, at this moment, she was.

Something deep down inside her told her that she had always known they would be lovers. She had resisted him with all her strength, but now the fighting was over.

CHAPTER NINE

The trouble was, she thought as she gazed in the mirror, her choices were limited: dresses or jeans and the rest of her clothes were shorts and T-shirts; everything else she had left behind in the London flat.

189

In the end, she decided on a slender calf-length skirt in a soft blue chenille, teamed with an ivory silk blouse with no sleeves and a very delicate neckline with tiny white embroidered butterflies sewn at the edges. Against her creamy skin-tone the contrast worked, but all the same she felt very nervous.

Was it because she had selected her silky underwear with even greater care? Blushing at her decision to wear lacy-topped ivory stockings on what was a rather warm evening, she told herself that it was to complement the pretty new low-heeled sandals she had bought, with their little golden fastenings.

As she bent to remove the pasta from the oven she heard the bell and jumped—as she always seemed to jump when she knew it was Bruno. Idiotic, of course, but all the same her pulses raced as she went to let him in. 'Smells and looks wonderful,' he said with a big grin as she opened the door.

'I hope you like pasta.' She laughed shyly, feeling a warm tide run over her as he stared at her. 'It has an accompanying sauce . . . Though I was silly—I didn't even ask you what you liked . . .'

'Come here!' He pulled her into his arms, effectively stopping her mindless babble. 'How I've longed to do this . . .' And he carried out his longing, his mouth covering hers with an intensity that left her no room to breathe. When she eventually did, she was aware that

190

he was leading her through the lounge towards the bedroom—no words were said, nor needed to be said. There was only the vague uncertainty in her mind that she had left the pasta on the hob to cool . . .

He hesitated in the hall. 'I'm not letting you out of my sight,' he threatened as they stood still. 'Which way'?'

She nodded to her little bedroom and the double bed which almost filled it. It was a sweet room with chintzy trimmings and had a beautiful window which overlooked the lane, and she could lie awake at night and hear all the comforting summer sounds.

'Oh, Frances . . . you look beautiful.' He took her tenderly in his arms. 'I want to unwrap you like a parcel, like a Christmas present.'

'It's a long way off,' she reminded him wryly, aware that his fingers had already begun to unfasten the small clip at the back of her blouse. 'Do you think you can wait?'

'I have no intention of waiting. I want you, Frances, and I want you now.'

'Then it seems I have no choice but to be unwrapped . . .'

He smiled as his mouth brushed her lips. 'Your hair is so long and thick,' he muttered as he lifted it away from the smooth material so she could wriggle out. As she stood there self-consciously in the dainty buff lace chemise a cluster of goose bumps covered her soft skin.

He bent his dark head to kiss them away.

She closed her eyes, slowly drifting into heaven. She felt she had wings as he lifted her bodily and sank with her to the bed. She found herself scrabbling at the buttons which closed his shirt, making a nervous effort to wrap her fingers around the leather belt, and he laughed, his fingers going over hers gently.

'Here, let me. .

He undid the solid black belt in one swift movement and soon his trousers were dispensed with almost in the same movement as her skirt, fluttering down beside the bed to the floor.

His eyes fastened to the slender length of the stockings that lay like velvet over her legs. For one second she was utterly embarrassed, her motive for putting them on this evening so transparent that she blushed.

'Sexy lady,' he breathed, running his fingers over them, undoing a dainty cream suspender. But the tenderness lasted only as long as his patience in undoing the other three, and as she helped him she felt his hands tremble, the delicate operation making them aware of how hungry they were for each other.

Stockings drawn slowly down her legs, lips brushing her skin in their wake, she groaned. His caresses were slow and tantalising and drove her crazy. Finally, when the last inch came off her toes, he nibbled each one with his teeth and she cried aloud, excitement choking in her throat as he slid upward over her body and silenced her with a long and hungry kiss.

'How many more layers?' he whispered in her ear as he buried his face in her hair.

She swallowed, lost in the heat of her passion. 'As many as you want . . .'

He cupped her breasts, kissed each rosy tip and drove her crazy again. Then his fingers wrapped around her thighs and brought her across his hips in one strong movement.

Under the waterfall of her hair they locked together in an embrace that sent them tumbling across the bed, limbs entwined, as the course of their lovemaking drove them to demand each other with long-anticipated greed.

In her oblivion she heard him whisper her name. She stroked the hard planes of his stomach and gasped at the extent of his desire for her.

'I love you, Frances. I think I've loved you from the first moment I saw you.'

She held his face in her fingers. 'Oh, darling, please don't say it if you're not sure.'

'Sure?' he groaned. 'I've waited long enough to say it.'

'Please understand,' she pleaded, 'I want to be loved for who I am . . .'

An angry growl came from his throat as he pushed her back. 'Damn it, Frances, how must I convince you?'

Could she believe it? Dared she believe

it? At this moment she wanted him too much to question, and with a reluctance to hear anything more, she covered his mouth and kissed him with a passion that drove him to pull her into the arch of his body and sigh her name. She whispered her own soft words of endearment, barely sure of what she was saying. His body was so beautiful, so honed, so perfectly proportioned—he delighted her with his eagerness to please, his strength and vitality and most of all his skilful lovemaking, which waited for her own lingering following.

'Oh, sweet girl,' he said softly, drawing her beneath him, cupping her small firm buttocks in his hands, gazing into her eyes with a burning fire in his own. 'Trust me.'

'Please,' she begged, thrusting her fingers into his hair, and he moved for a few seconds apart from her. She realised that he was being thoughtful about the safety of their lovemaking—though for herself she had forgotten, selfishly lost in pleasure.

Soon they were beyond words again, their bodies moving as if for all time they had been meant to be together. There was no past or future. No ghost of Lindsay. Nothing to stand between them, nothing outside the room—just this moment.

*   *   *

They sat up in bed in the early morning
194

propped by pillows, with a very pale dawn breaking across the summer sky. Frances sighed, a feeling of sublime exhaustion filling her as she nestled into his arms 'What time must you leave?' she asked, her eyes lingering on the long shape of his body next to her, filling out her bed so easily that it was as though he had always been there, sleeping beside her.

'I'm not going back to the house,' he whispered, nuzzling his chin into her hair.

'Won't Rosa expect you?'

He chuckled softly. 'I'm a big boy now, remember?'

She laughed too and lay back, content to look at him, relishing every brown contour, every muscle and sinew, her eye tracing the stubble that had formed overnight on his jaw and made him look so piratical.

'What about shaving—fresh clothes?'

He snuggled down beside her. 'In my over-night bag at the bottom of your staircase.'

'Why leave it there?'

'I was only supposed to be coming for dinner, remember? What would you have said if I'd bundled the bag in front of me last night?'

'Oh, I'd probably have booted you back out again.'

'Hard-hearted woman!' He kissed her nose. 'You won't get rid of me that easily!'

She lifted herself up on one elbow. 'Is that a

threat or a promise?'

He trailed a finger across her cheek. 'A promise, my darling . . . because I'm in love with you. Frances, I've never been more serious in my life. I want us to be married.'

She looked at him incredulously. 'Don't tease, Bruno.'

'I'm not. I'm utterly serious—I told you. I want you for my wife. I want us to be together for the rest of our lives. All you have to say is yes.'

She struggled up, pushing her hands against his chest. 'Bruno—'

'Darling, do you love me?'

She could see the determination in his eyes, hear it in his voice, and, defeated, she nodded slowly. 'Yes, I love you. I love you dearly.'

He hugged her to him and she felt his deep, relieved intake of breath. 'Then just say yes—it's all that matters. Hell, I'm no damn bargain, I'll agree—not at thirty-six with a ten-year-old son and a frantic practice—but I promise I shall make you a happy woman . . . a very happy woman, if only you'll let me try.'

She wanted to believe him so much. But did he really know his own mind? Were the ghosts of the past still there, hidden at the moment by the physical pleasure they gave one another? They had just spent a wonderful, incredible night making love. To ask her to marry him now . . .?

'Bruno, can we discuss this later?' she asked

softly.

'Like when?'

'Like when I have some clothes on and I can think properly, without you moving up and down beside me!'

He grinned 'But that's my technique—that's my big plan. To persuade you to say yes to me whilst I have you at a disadvantage.'

She traced a finger over his lips. 'I'm grateful for your proposal—and as it happens, neither the practice or Jack comes into the equation. I'm addicted to them both. But marriage? Marriage is something else.'

'I know,' he said softly. 'Believe me, I know it. Lord, Frances, after what happened between Lindsay and I—'

Suddenly tears smarted in her eyes. She tried to hide them. Didn't he know? Didn't he understand that Lindsay—always Lindsay—was precisely the reason she couldn't marry him?

'Darling, don't turn away from me. What's wrong?'

She reached for his hand and surreptitiously wiped her eyes. She held his fingers to her mouth and, kissing them, shook her head, wishing that she could be honest enough to say that she did not want to be loved in Lindsay's image.

Even if he thought he was over his dead wife there would be constant daily reminders— shoes she would be stepping into which

197

weren't hers, a role filled previously by a woman extinguished before her time.

Oh, she had thought about Lindsay so often. She knew every scenario by heart. She'd imagined making love in that big double bed where Lindsay had slept with him. She'd visualised trying to fit in with Jack and Rosa—a bereaved child and a brave mother, who, much as they might like her on a friendly basis, might come to resent the intrusion into their lives.

'Is it him?' he suddenly demanded.

'Who?' She blinked at the pressure of his fingers turning her chin towards him. 'Greg? Of course not.'

'Frances, I'm not interrogating you about your past. But if you still have feelings for the guy, then I want to know exactly what I'm up against.'

She saw the same expression in his eyes as must have been in hers over the past few weeks. The piercing, hateful emotion of jealousy, which she understood only too well. If only she could tell Bruno that her relationship with Greg had never come close to being what she had with him! Greg had been her only lover, but his different postings had kept them apart and often, when they'd been reunited, there had never been any eagerness between them. His mind had always been on the next assignment. She had recognised that it was more of a drug to him than their lovemaking.

'Frances, I must know.'

She threaded her arms around his neck and snuggled up to him. Their bodies melded together and she heard his indrawn sigh. 'Darling, Greg means nothing to me any more. I was hurt . . . yes—terribly at the time. But it really is over now. I promise you.'

He searched her eyes and nodded slowly. 'Then it's Lindsay, isn't it?' he said flatly.

'I can't help it,' she whispered, ashamed of herself 'If I didn't look so much like her. If she hadn't hurt you so badly. If—'

He, pulled her towards him and she was not surprised to see small white lines of anger tightening his mouth. 'You're obsessed with her, Frances,' he growled. 'What do I have to do to convince you?'

Those hurt, dark eyes made her feel hungry for him all over again. She buried her head in his chest. He held her very gently, but she could feel the angry vibrations running under his skin.

'Kiss me,' he commanded her, and drew up her face.

She responded to his seeking lips with a fierce desire of her own. She needed him more than ever—and she needed him now, here in her bed, where they were safe.

*   *   *

At six the alarm went off, just as they had succumbed to sleep. She awoke, her head resting in the crook of his shoulder, his arm across the jut of her hip.

She prised herself away from him and struggled to silence the alarm. He caught his arms around her waist and pulled her down.

'Don't go . . .'

Wantonly she revelled in his arousal. 'We can't,' she whispered, kissing him, her lips bruised from the long hours of lovemaking. Not if you want breakfast and a shower—'

'I want you.' He kissed her too, pushing back the long tendrils of hair from her sleepy face.

'And I want you.'

'Then stay.'

She sighed. 'You know it's impossible. If we were both late this morning, there would be no end to the gossip. And besides, the Range Rover is parked in the lane.'

'You want me to move it before any of your neighbours see, I suppose?'

She laughed softly. 'I want you to arrive at the surgery on time.'

'So that no one suspects!'

'If you like.'

'But I don't give a damn who suspects. In fact, I want everyone to know. I want the whole world to—'

She hauled herself up through the tangle of sheets, sliding on her robe. 'Bruno, don't.

200

Please let's not go over it all again.'

He rolled on his back with a deep sigh. She wanted to slide back in with him, run her fingers through that wonderful mat of thick glossy hair curling over his chest. He was the most delicious man she had ever laid eyes on, and he made love to her with such perfection.

'Come on, lazy bones. You take the shower first and I'll cook breakfast.'

'Has anyone ever told you you look like an angel first thing in the morning?'

She giggled. 'You're incorrigible.'

'And you are beautiful, Frances Duncan.'

He, was staring at her with a look that made her quiver from head to toe. No wonder she had let herself go last night. She could willingly have repeated the performance . . . but she resisted the temptation. 'Two eggs?' It was the only sane thing she could think of to say.

He grinned. 'Don't change the subject.'

She threw a pillow at him. 'See you at the breakfast table!'

In the kitchen, she breathed a deep sigh and swiftly cracked two large eggs into the pan. And, to her relief, soon there was movement in the bathroom accompanied by a breezy whistling.

Breakfast made, he arrived in a short white hand-towel, his naked body glimmering with a wet sheen of water.

'Show-off!' She darted out of his reach as she pushed him down in a chair, averting

201

her eyes from the indecent sight of strong, muscular legs and damp chest flagrantly exhibiting themselves at her table.

'Eat!' She pushed a fork into his hand.

'What about you?'

'I'm showering! And the shower is off-limits for the next fifteen minutes!'

He shouted something rude from the kitchen.

It was good having him around, she thought as she stroked luxurious shampoo into her hair and wallowed in its passage down the length of her body. Almost too good. How could falling in love be so wonderful and so painful at the same time?

There was something sublime in having him all to herself over the next week, without the rush of him having to hurry home. There was also something naughtily exciting about keeping their relationship secret. It felt as though it was just the two of them against the world—a world of work and pressure and discipline. And retreating to her flat during lunch hours or stolen moments, or when he wasn't on call, was blissful. She didn't even have to worry about Rosa being alone, because, being the perceptive woman Rosa was, she had taken herself off to the Lakes to visit her friend.

Jack phoned the flat twice, but Frances didn't say that his father was with her. Once it was quite late, around nine, and she and

Bruno had just made love on the settee and were lounging on the floor on cushions in the process of feeding each other long lengths of spaghetti, too lazy to sit at the table. She felt a bit underhand when she spoke to Jack. She wanted to tell him that his father was there with her, but Bruno shook his head.

'He wouldn't think we were necessarily up to anything,' she protested afterwards, winding spaghetti thoughtfully over her fork.

Bruno laughed as he took the fork from her, cast their plates aside and pulled her into his arms. No, but he would want to think it.' He looked at her soberly. 'You must know how Jack feels about you? He adores you.'

She sighed and he held up his hands. 'OK. I'm not pushing the subject. It's just that if he knows I'm around here, he'll put two and two together.' He gave her a wicked grin. 'Why don't you come home with me this weekend? If he rings then, he won't be surprised to hear you. And we can swim . . . laze the days away . . .'

'And what about Saturday surgery?' she asked in amazement.

'Tristan will swap.'

'You've asked him?'

He nodded, pulling her closer. 'Of course I have. Did you think I intended to work on the one weekend we have the house to ourselves?'

She studied the remains of their meal. 'Oh, I'm not sure . . .'

He gave her a tomato-ish kiss. 'You don't have a choice in the matter, Frances Duncan. You're coming on Friday night and staying till Monday morning and that's that.'

She couldn't help but smile. 'Bully!'

He nodded. 'I've got to be where you're concerned.'

*　　　*　　　*

On Friday, she packed a case and stowed it in the boot of the Clio feeling very machiavellian. She was excited, much more than she had expected, but she was also nervous. Somehow she had it fixed in her mind that the house was Lindsay's territory. In a strange way she felt she would be confronting Lindsay there.

She tried to reassure herself as she walked into Cherry Grove. Hadn't she harboured preposterous thoughts about Suzie Collins and Meg Fellows? And she had maligned Bruno simply because of gossip. Now she knew there was nothing in it, she could actually look at Suzie and Meg in a completely different light. And wouldn't it be the same when she came to terms with Lindsay Quillan?

The fact that she was dead, though, still seemed to make little or no difference, she decided morbidly, unable to free herself of the mood! Jealousy still had its sting. Perhaps even a worse one if the subject of the sting wasn't made of flesh and bone.

'Frances!' Gill called to her as she walked in the surgery. 'Just a mo!' She hurried out from behind the desk and pressed an envelope into her hand. 'Dr Quillan asked me to give you this. He was called away the moment he stepped in this morning—that patient of his who had the angiography?'

Frances frowned. 'Gabriel Bally?'

'He suffered a coronary thrombosis last night.'

'In the hospital?' Frances was deeply shocked.

'Apparently so. Anyway, Dr Quillan went over straight away. He asked me to let you know and pass this on to you.'

Frances nodded. 'Thanks, Gill. Any more messages?'

'Only one in the nurse's book. Madjur Rasti The health visitor has asked if you can meet her there at ten.'

Frances felt her stomach kick. She knew it! It was going to be one of those days. She'd thought it might just be her apprehension on a personal level, but sometimes gut instinct warned that it was going to be a miserable day—and she had the sinking feeling that this was going to be one of them.

She said thank you to Gill again, collected her things and left the practice, praying that she'd be wrong about Madjur for a start, for she had come home from the bursa op last week and Louise Lambert had made a

205

preliminary visit.

In the car, Frances slit open the envelope and read in Bruno's clear writing, 'Missed you lots last night. Don't forget to come straight home for supper at the house! Love B.'

She smiled and folded the note back. He had been on call last night and she had missed him too. Her bed had been lonely without him. She realised that it would always be lonely now—every single thing in the flat reminded her of him.

Louise greeted her as she arrived at Madjur's. 'I've just put the kettle on. Glad you could make it.'

Frances smiled and went into the front room, where Madjur lay on the familiar old bed-settee. She looked terribly thin.

'How are you?' she asked gently as she sat beside her.

'I had the bursa done. Now they're talking about doing hip and shoulder joint replacements.'

'How do you feel about more surgery?'

Madjur shook her head. 'Not very happy. In fact, I've decided I don't want any more operations.'

Louise came in with a tray of tea. She put it on the table in front of them and sat down on a chair. 'Mrs Rasti told you? Well, it's either replacements or we shall have to consider a team approach. Physio, hydrotherapy, dietitian, OT and obviously drug therapy.

You're, on Indocid now, aren't you?'

Madjur nodded. 'The hospital put me on that. But I have these stomach upsets all the time.'

The health visitor glanced at Frances. 'Perhaps you can have a word with Dr Quillan? There are other alternatives, aren't there?'

Frances glanced at Madjur's careplan and saw that she had already tried Brufen and Naprosyn. Bruno had once mentioned D-Penicillamine, but the benefits only showed up over a period of months, and it was not unknown for there to be side-effects too. All in all, replacement joints would be the best alternative if the consultant had advised them, but she could see by Madjur's expression that getting her back into hospital again was going to be difficult—if not impossible.

They all talked for a while about the alternatives. But by eleven they were no closer to persuading Madjur into having surgery. The health visitor packed away her case and had a few quick words with Frances before she left.

Going back into the room, Frances removed the tea things and put a knife and fork on the coffee-table for when the meals on wheels lady arrived.

'I don't like to leave you like this,' she said on a sigh. Will you be able to manage the loo?'

Madjur nodded. 'I've the commode, thanks. And I'll wash in the kitchen. I can get myself out there but it takes time.'

Frances smiled and decided to try one last time. 'You're very brave, Madjur. But you know, replacement joints might be the answer. Isn't it an opportunity to grasp whilst you can?'

Her patient closed her eyes wearily. 'I've had enough of them pulling me around. And they can't guarantee anything. No, Frances, I don't want to go back into hospital again.' She suddenly opened her eyes. 'Did you ever send that letter?'

Blushing, Frances nodded. 'You've not had a reply?'

'Not a thing.' Her small body quivered. 'Still, I didn't expect to. It was just clutching at straws. But thanks all the same.'

Feeling hopelessly inadequate, Frances made Madjur as comfortable as she could and took her leave. Not that she could get Madjur out of her mind, and her problems stayed with her for the rest of the day.

Back at the surgery she saw Bruno. He smiled at her across a busy Reception and she smiled back, aware that the girls were all too ready to put an interpretation on the merest glance.

A few minutes later he deliberately collided with her in the hall and she found herself laughing. 'You idiot!' she whispered as he grappled with the papers he had clumsily knocked out of her hands.

'And you're coming home with me tonight,

don't forget!' he whispered back, eyeing the corridor both ways. 'Here, come with me—I need to talk to you.'

'Haven't you a patient?'

He grinned 'I have now. Come and talk to Dr Quillan.'

She giggled and followed him sedately along to his room, not daring to look over at Reception.

When the door closed behind them he pushed her back against it, flung her papers on the desk and kissed her so hard that she struggled for breath.

'Dr Quillan!' She laughed softly. 'What kind of treatment is this?'

He kissed her again, his tongue pushing between her teeth, his lovely mobile lips covering her shocked mouth. 'Alternative, as a matter of fact. And I'm finding it very, very effective . . .'

She looked up into his face and leant her head back on the door, sighing. 'We're going to get caught one day, you know.'

He nodded roguishly. 'I hope so. Then you'll have to make an honest man out of me.'

She pushed him away. 'So that's your evil plan?'

He watched her walk to the chair and sit primly in it. 'Oh, no.' He leered, straightening his crooked tie. 'I've a variety of evil plans in mind. For instance—'

'Come and sit down and behave,' she

interrupted him wisely, just as the intercom on the desk shrieked.

He answered it with a growl. Suzie Collins informed him that he was half an hour behind and he told her to give him five minutes.

Frances laughed. 'You're just a tease.'

He arched dark eyebrows. 'Say that again this evening and we shall see! Now . . . to work. I saw Gabriel today. You know he suffered a coronary thrombosis?'

Frances sighed and nodded. 'How is he?'

'He's in Intensive and will be for another twenty-four hours. There is no sign of disturbance to heart rhythm at the moment and they have the pain under control. They've got him on anticoagulant, but the angiography shows that we'll have to consider surgery— possibly coronary artery bypass grafting. He's a nonsmoker, thank God, and was quite fit until the hernia began. The trouble is, he's reluctant to go ahead . . . for some reason he won't discuss with me. Until we get his co-operation there's not a thing we can do.'

Frances sat back in the chair. She knew exactly why Gabriel Bally didn't want treatment! She opened her mouth and shut it again.

'Frances?' He was staring at her. 'Is there something you want to say?'

'I'm not sure,' she sighed. She lifted her blue eyes hesitantly. 'Well, I suppose I should. It might be important.'

'Anything.' Bruno frowned. 'Anything you think might help.'

She said reluctantly, 'I can only say what I saw. Gabriel may be worrying about leaving his wife. After all, an operation and then time to recuperate—it will all take time. And an enforced absence . . .'

'Go on.'

'Well, I saw Petra Bally one evening. She was with another man—a much younger man.' She described briefly what she had seen at the pub as impartially as she could. When she'd finished, she shrugged. 'I suppose Gabriel is concerned the affair might develop in his absence, or that she couldn't cope with the prospect of looking after him.'

To her surprise, Bruno looked as though a steamroller had run over him. His mouth thinned into a straight, angry line and the lovely brown eyes which usually radiated such warmth turned cold.

'I see,' he muttered under his breath, staring at her. 'How stupid of me. I should have guessed there was something. And you knew all along?'

Frances was hurt by his tone of voice. 'I knew, yes. But I thought it would serve no purpose gossiping. And there was the chance you may have thought it was sour grapes on my part . . . in view of Petra Bally's complaint.'

He looked at her for a long while and then, astounding her, said between gritted teeth,

'Well, you were wrong. You should have told me. But then, I suppose you saw no problem arising from the woman having a little fling behind her husband's back? If the boot had been on the other foot no doubt you'd have informed me immediately.'

Frances could not believe what she had just heard, nor understand the swift change in atmosphere. Only a few moments ago they had been laughing and joking lovingly, and now he was sitting there accusing her of something completely irrational and unfair.

'Do you honestly think I would condone an affair—on either side?' she gasped, wondering if she was talking to the same man who had kissed her so passionately only moments before.

'Would you?' He was staring at her with such coldness that she felt a shiver of ice down her spine.

'Of course I wouldn't!'

His mouth jerked. 'Gabriel Bally is an ill man. She's young enough to be his daughter. She's attractive, intelligent and both you and I know they have a problem within the marriage—a problem that won't rectify itself within the near future in Gabriel's case. You mean to tell me you don't think that's reason enough for the woman to look elsewhere for attention?'

Frances rose to her feet. 'You should be asking Petra Bally, not me.' Her cheeks flushed with anger. 'I've told you how I feel about marriage. The vows people make are forever—for richer for poorer and in sickness or health, hackneyed though it may sound these days. I can't answer for your patient's behaviour—and I don't intend to stand here and be cross-questioned on her behalf!' She marched to the door. 'Now, if you're quite finished—Dr Quillan?'

She choked out the last two words. His face was a blur in front of her. Tears of injustice pricked hotly behind her eyes, but she managed to hold them back as she left the room, pulling the door hard behind her.

She nearly knocked over Gill, who was passing. The receptionist stared after her as she stumbled along the hall to the cloakrooms.

What a horrible, hateful thing to say to her. And to accuse her of deliberately condoning the affair when all she had tried to do was limit the gossip that was already flying around his precious practice!

In the loo, she dabbed at her eyes.

More angry than hurt now, she laid wet palms over her burning cheeks. She took a deep breath and sighed, a tiny sob coming up. Why? she asked herself. Why turn on her? Then suddenly she knew.

Because he was confusing her with Lindsay!

It was Lindsay who had deceived him, and he still suffered the wounds of that deception. She had been right when she had guessed that

213

Lindsay was still not out of his system—oh, so right.

After ten minutes, she had calmed down enough to go to the office. She retrieved her case and left, and drove home in the Clio, forcing herself to be careful as she drove, carefully containing the mixed emotions which bubbled fiercely under the surface of her control.

When she got there she climbed out and went to the back of the car and pulled out her overnight case. Well, it had turned out to be a black Friday after all.

She slid her key into the lock and found herself hauling her weak legs and seemingly extra heavy load up the little flight of stairs. The first thing she saw when she entered the front room was his sweater. It hung over a chair where she always kept it, often laying it around her shoulders when he wasn't there, the smell of lemony-lime making up for his absence.

She dropped her armful, sank onto the settee and stared at the sweater. Then she held her head in her hands and let the tears fall.

CHAPTER TEN

The phone rang, as she'd guessed it would.

She ignored it, showered and unpacked her

case, half expecting a knock at the front door, half wanting it. But it didn't come.

The next morning she threw on denims and a white shirt and omitted breakfast. She drove out early into Cerne Carey, had coffee in a busy little restaurant, shopped for groceries at Mrs Dean's and spent the rest of her Saturday wandering around the town, unable to concentrate on anything and yet unable to return home.

This was to have been such a special weekend. Her mind turned to the strawberry-pink house set amidst its green wrapper of summer foliage. Bruno would be there on his own. She was tempted . . . but she resisted. After all, it was he who had accused her so unfairly, not the other way around.

Half-heartedly eating a cream tea in a café in the little cobbled shopping precinct, she gazed out of the shop window, listening to the chatter around her. How could he accuse her as he had? And why so suddenly . . . when only moments before . . . ?

Stop it, she told herself, sighing heavily. Come on Frances Duncan, you'd better get yourself home. You can't stay out all night.

But it was almost seven before she drove into Bow Lane. The back seat was filled with small green plants for the window box—her idea for occupying what promised to be a depressingly empty Sunday.

A sleek red car with a black convertible

hood was parked outside her front door. She had to squeeze the Clio in behind it, muttering under her breath as she pulled on the brake and finally cut the engine.

She was loaded up with bags and the two trays from the garden nursery, and whilst trying to balance them in her arms and unlock her front door at the same time one of the trays slipped.

A pair of large hands caught it and popped one fallen shoot back into the loamy soil.

'Well, now. I didn't know gardening was an interest of yours.' The voice sent her eyes flying up in shock to its owner.

Her mouth fell open in astonishment. 'You're looking terrific, Fran.'

She gulped, blinking to make sure that it wasn't an apparition. 'Greg!'

He bent from his tall height to kiss her, fully on the lips.

She craned back her neck, realising that his free hand had slipped around her waist. 'Wh-what are you doing here?'

'Looking for you, of course. You are an elusive lady. This is the third time I've called today.'

Frances stared at the wide shoulders under the tan shirt, at the erect posture and the slightly bent close-cropped fair head, her mind taking in the fact that this was the man who had once occupied such a special place in her life.

216

'But . . . but how did you find me?'

He grinned. 'If you'll let me in, I'll tell you.'

She realised that she still hadn't opened up. Her fingers faltering, she pushed open the door and he followed her. She didn't even think whether or not she should be letting him in as he helped her with her bags and they ascended the flight of stairs.

He began telling her of how he'd called at the flat in London, found she wasn't there and how the caretaker, recognising him, had finally agreed to give him her new address.

'But I told her not to give it to anyone!' Frances protested as she dumped her things and stared at the virtual stranger who had promptly made himself comfortable on the settee.

'Yes, but she saw it was me,' Greg told her confidently. 'And we were going out for two years, Frances.' He laughed. 'Or have you forgotten?'

She was not amused. 'No, I haven't forgotten.' And she hadn't forgotten the long months of heartache afterwards either, when he'd blithely flown off into the sunset without so much as one letter from the Gulf

'Coffee?' she asked politely. 'I'm afraid I've nothing stronger.'

'Coffee—and your company . . . fine!' He gave her the smile which she remembered had once made her heart beat faster. Now it left her cold. She hurried away, hoping that the expression of distaste wasn't evident on her face. She made coffee in the kitchen, wondering why he had turned up, and as she did so the phone rang in the other room. Before she could get there, Greg had answered it.

She walked in to find him frowning. 'Someone hung up,' he said, and took the mug of coffee.

She folded her arms in a defensive action across her white shirt. His eyes dropped to the soft shape of her breasts revealed beneath the smooth material and she blushed. 'Would you mind telling me why you've called?'

He put the coffee down and hung a sunburned forearm on the window shelf. 'Nice place,' he murmured, turning his face to stare down the lane. 'Do you live here alone?'

She couldn't believe it! He was interrogating her! He had the nerve to walk back into her life after over a year and seemed to think he had a right to know everything. 'Greg . . . what do you want?'

He looked back at her. 'I would have thought that was obvious.' The invitation was plainly written in his eyes. Suddenly she remembered how much he'd once meant to her . . . He was attractive and tanned, his fair hair even blonder than it used to be from months in the sun, his light blue eyes narrowing as he studied her. 'You're looking lovelier than ever, Fran.'

'Greg, I have other things to do . . .'

'Such as?'

She stiffened. 'That's my business.'

'Why do I get the impression you're not putting yourself out to be very friendly?'

She gasped, her blue eyes darkening angrily. 'You walked out of my life without any qualms, Greg. You chose the Army and you dumped me—why should I be friendly?'

He laughed softly and ambled towards her. 'Still annoyed?' His strong hands suddenly tightened on her arms. 'Well, there's nothing we can't put right, you know. I'm leaving the Army. Had an offer from a friend in the city who needs technical expertise like mine. It's a good offer, and I thought you and I—'

Angrily, she tried to shrug him off 'Greg, what you do with your life now is not my concern. It's too late for us—much too late. Please let me go.'

'Oh, Fran . . . come off your high horse!' He pulled her closer and bent his head. She knew what he was about to do, but she turned her head sideways and the kiss landed on her ear.

She tried to push him away, her pulses racing in alarm. 'Stop it, Greg. Let me go!'

'Fran . . . come here . . .'

'I suggest you do exactly as the lady says and let her go,' said a deep voice from the open door.

The fingers around her arms slowly dropped, and she almost fell back as Greg released her. 'Are you OK?' Bruno asked her in a low voice.

She nodded. 'Greg was . . . just leaving.'

Her guest stared at her, his colour deepening aggressively as Bruno walked in front of him and stood beside her, effectively separating them. She felt the physical animosity between the two men.

'Close the door behind you,' Bruno growled, his brown gaze as hard as nails. After a moment's hesitation Greg cast her one last disparaging glance, gave a contemptuous snarl and headed out of the room.

'Are you sure you're all right?' Bruno asked her.

She nodded shakily. 'Y-yes.'

There was a loud slam from the bottom of the stairs and then the savage roar of the red car out in the lane revving up and screeching away.

She let out her breath for a moment and closed her eyes. When she opened them, somehow she was encompassed in a strong pair of arms Bruno held her tightly, the solid feel of his body making her swallow with relief as she slid her arms around him. 'Oh, darling,' she mumbled into his shoulder, 'I've missed you.'

'Thank God for that,' he breathed, his chest rising under her cheek. 'I wasn't sure if—' He stopped, prising her away from him and staring into her eyes. 'The front door was open when

I arrived, and when I came up and saw him holding you—'

'I shouldn't have let him in.' Every ounce of energy was drained from her body. Her eyes were moist with tears as she stared up at him. 'I was a fool.'

He bent to capture her mouth and a thrill went through her like an electric shock. 'No, I've been the fool,' he whispered achingly. 'What I said to you yesterday . . . it was unforgivable.'

She ran her fingers into his hair. 'Oh, darling!'

He pulled her body into the curve of his; making her gasp as she realised how much he needed her, running his hands down over her small, neat bottom, flicking his fingers to the waistband of her jeans, unwrapping the soft folds of her shirt from her hot skin.

'Oh God, Frances,' he groaned, 'we've wasted so much time . . .' And before she could lead him to the bedroom he had picked her up in his arms and was making swift work of the journey with his long strides, kicking the door shut behind them. The echoing sound was wonderfully exciting to her ears as he began to make passionate love to her in the warmth of the sultry, sexy summer's evening.

*　　　*　　　*

The rest of the weekend was spent in bed.

221

Her bed. Not because she made excuses not to go home with him again, but because they were just too cosy to move. Luckily she had everything in that they needed from her expedition to Mrs Dean's—not that much of it went on the table. Most of it ended up on their knees, either in bed or on their laps in the front room; where they lounged on the floor against the sofa.

She got all explanations out of the way first—after all, she couldn't just ignore the fact that Greg had been trying to kiss her! And after that she hoped they might discuss Lindsay, bring the subject out into the open, but Bruno somehow had the knack of glossing over it and making such wonderful love to her that she'd forgotten by the time they surfaced.

One question did come up. One she had been thinking about herself. It was in the early hours of Monday morning, when she lay awake in his arms, their bodies expended with the pleasures of the night.

'Making babies,' he mumbled, and she laughed softly.

'Is that an observation or a suggestion?' She was joking, of course, but he was quiet, and she rolled into him, snuggling up to his warm body. 'Bruno, you're taking precautions, so there isn't a need to worry, is there?'

His lips came down to kiss the top of her head. 'No, not in that sense. But eventually we are going to have to think about them.'

'Them?'

'Well, we shall want more than one. Jack will be at school. There will be a big age-gap and I've never much fancied the idea of only children.'

'Bruno, we aren't even married!'

'And whose fault is that?'

She eased herself up on one elbow and stared into his shadowed face. 'You're racing ahead!'

He brought her into his arms. 'I've a perfect right to,' he told her moodily. 'We love each other and we need to be married before having kids—though, again, that's probably contrary to popular belief these days—so what the hell are we waiting for? Frances, when are you going to see reason?'

He sighed, taking her into his arms and drawing her naked body closer, and ran his hands down the smooth plane of her back. She felt the thrill of his body and groaned. How easy it would be to give in—if only she were sure. He kissed her neck, smoothing his lips down the softness of her throat, then rolled her back on the pillow and eased his fingers in between the silkiness of her thighs, drawing a gasp from her throat. 'Come here,' he whispered gently, 'you stubborn little witch. I can't be angry with you for long.'

'I'm not stubborn.'

'Yes, you are.'

'You see, we're disagreeing again.'

He pulled her closer. 'And we are just about to make up. Like this . . .'

His body moved with such perfect skill that she was lost, abandoned, easy prey to the soft persuasion of his lips. Half an hour ago she'd been satiated, exhausted with pleasure, unable to imagine another floodtide of desire encompassing her as it did now, thrusting up from her toes into the pit of her stomach. The moment strained between them. It seemed to last a second and an eternity all at once.

Her body fluttered from the heights like a bird planing down on the wind, and she descended from the climax of their love breathless in his arms, loving him with such a love that it filled all of her. And yet still the doubts remained.

*   *   *

Monday was the hottest day of the year.

Jack rang his father at home to say that Christina and Uncle Nigel were taking him sailing, and Bruno seemed pleased. 'At least it'll get him away from the blessed machines,' he told Frances wryly the following morning. 'Christina has asked me if he can stay another week. They're taking the boat out of Southampton.'

Frances smiled across her little breakfast table. 'Great. How does Jack feel about sailing?'

Bruno looked up and grinned 'I get the feeling he'd much rather be here at home, picnicking with you.'

She laughed. 'The novelty would soon wear off.'

He smiled. 'I doubt it.' He thought for a moment. 'Rosa will want him back some time in early August. We've the uniform business to resolve.'

'Harrington Hall uniform, you mean?'

Bruno half choked over his coffee. 'A bit late now to plan otherwise!'

She shrugged. 'Not necessarily. There's a good day-school near Cerne Carey. I've several patients who have sons there. They've good exam results and a marvellous reputation . . .'

'Rosa didn't put you up to this, by any chance?'

She flushed. 'We have discussed it . . .'

'Frances . . . Jack has special needs. He's an introvert and shy, and he's obsessed by machines. He needs much more than I can provide as a single parent. That is . . .' He gazed up at her with a strangely defeated look. 'I can't expect Rosa to cancel out the rest of her life for us. She needs her own time and space. Oh, hell, I've looked at it all ways round—and this is the best way.'

She held her breath. 'Even if I agree to marry you?'

The silence snapped electrically in the small

kitchen. 'You'd say yes to me for Jack's sake?'

She sat quite still, wondering what she did mean. That was how it had sounded . . .

He stood up, grazing the chair angrily back across the floor. 'As a matter of fact, Frances, that's the last reason I'd have you say yes to me. I'm not looking for a surrogate mother for Jack. Did you really think that's why I asked you to marry me?'

'I—'

He walked away angrily and she heard the door slam. She ached to run after him. But she didn't. After all, wasn't his question valid? Wasn't that exactly what she had suspected?

'Oh, hell,' she breathed, lowering her face into her hands.

It was the first time she'd seen Sarah Clark for weeks. And the change in her was significant.

'Come in, come in!' She welcomed Frances and led her into the lounge, where baby Freddie kicked in his little chair. His sister was sitting beside him on the floor, playing with an assortment of toys.

'Joanna, this is Nurse Duncan,' Sarah introduced, and then she laughed. 'A bit long-winded that, isn't it? May we call you Frances?'

'Anything you like!' Frances was relieved to feel the ease of tension in the air. Meg Fellows had suggested she call to keep abreast of the case, knowing that Frances had taken an interest from the first. Now she found mother and children much more relaxed, and little Freddie was gurgling away, fatter and happier.

Without prompting Sarah told her how Meg Fellows had helped her with the postnatal depression. As she had experienced the problem herself, Sarah had related to her immediately, and in the weeks since had been able to talk out her feelings until now she felt almost back to normal.

'It began with what Dr Fellows explained was "third-day blues",' she recounted as they sat and played with the children. 'I was weepy and kept bursting into tears after Freddie's birth, and I felt so guilty. Instead of talking about it, I tried to hide it, and that was the worst thing I could have done. It was compounded by Freddie's illness. I felt he was sick because I didn't love him as much as I loved Joanna, and that he was punishing me by crying all the time. It was a vicious circle.

'Until I met someone who had experienced the same thing, I felt so responsible for his sickness! Then Dr Fellows explained what she had been through and slowly things began to click back into perspective again. I thought if a doctor had experienced it too, I couldn't be such a bad person after all.'

Frances nodded, remembering how Bruno had instinctively recognised that Meg would be the right physician for Sarah.

'I've Dr Quillan to thank too,' Sarah added

swiftly, 'for putting me in touch with Dr Fellows. But he's not a woman, bless him, and he hasn't suffered postnatal depression.' She paused. 'It's wonderful how they all work as a kind of team, isn't it?'

Frances swallowed on a pang of guilt. 'Yes, we're fortunate at Cerne Carey. Cherry Grove is a good practice—very good. Is there anything I can help you with today?'

Sarah giggled as she took Freddie from his seat and pushed the heavy, wriggling child into Frances's arms. 'You tell me!'

Frances widened her eyes as she cuddled him. 'What are you feeding him—steak and chips?'

Young Joanna burst out laughing, and soon all four of them were in fits of giggles as even little Freddie joined in the joke, chuckling and blowing bubbles.

When Frances left, she thought of the contrast between this household and the one she was going to. Here was a real happy ending, but Madjur Rasti's problems seemed insoluble. If Madjur wouldn't consider replacement joints then there was cause for little optimism with such a disabling disease.

It just didn't seem fair sometimes. There were three young lives all blossoming in the Clark household—if only a little of the happiness could rub off into this one.

It was a wish which was to be granted as the door opened and a younger version of Madjur stood there. In fact, Sarah had to blink several times to see if she hadn't imagined it.

'Nurse Duncan? Come in, please,' invited the young girl politely. She was beautiful, with dark glossy eyes and long black hair, and she wore a long sari of blue and gold.

Frances stepped in and held out her hand. 'Is it Serena?'

The girl laughed softly . . . 'Yes. Thank you for your letter. If it wasn't for you, I shouldn't be here.'

Frances's next shock was to find Madjur not lying on the bed-settee, but sitting in an easy chair. The place looked as clean as a whistle and there was a lovely smell as an incense stick burned on the fireplace.

'Oh, Frances, thank you.' Madjur held out her hands.

Frances took them and saw real happiness in Madjur's eyes, so unexpected that she found tears pricking her own. 'I can't believe this, Madjur! Serena is here?'

The three women laughed and Madjur nodded. 'She has been wonderful. A whole week she has been here, looking after me. Her father and grandparents didn't realise how my illness had worsened until they read your letter. They rang me from Delhi to ask if I would like Serena to come to England for the summer. I couldn't believe it!'

'Oh, that's wonderful, Madjur. I'm so pleased they understood and sympathised.'

Frances gazed at Serena and saw how Madjur would have looked in her youth. Indian women were so beautiful, and very graceful, and as she glanced back at the older woman some of that loveliness had begun to sparkle again in Madjur's eyes.

It was far too hot for tea, so Serena prepared cold drinks and brought them in on a tray. She helped her mother take her medication and Frances saw how gentle she was—not afraid of Madjur's illness at all, but genuinely pleased to be helping.

'I have had a big surprise,' Madjur explained excitedly. 'In the time Serena has been here we have had so much to talk about. She is going to become a doctor and hopes to come to England to study!'

Frances gripped her hand. 'Fabulous, Madjur!'

Her patient nodded and the tears crept down her cheeks—tears of joy, she was quick to explain as Frances unearthed her tissues and shared them around.

'My mother is considering having the treatment advised by Dr Quillan and Dr Ben Carter,' Serena said at last. 'We've talked about it and I think she has made up her mind.'

Frances breathed a sigh of relief. The prospect of surgery would not be so daunting whilst Serena was here. 'You won't be sorry, Madjur,' Frances said delightedly. 'After all, there's so much to look forward to now.'

It was, Frances decided, a red-letter day. She lingered with the Rastis far longer than she had planned, and when she finally left she was bursting to tell Bruno, who was, as far as she knew, unaware of the developments. After the way they had separated this morning, with words spoken in anger, it would be so wonderful to have this good news to tell him.

She could either drive back to the surgery and perhaps catch him there, or wait until he called in at the flat this evening. The temptation was too great to resist, and she drove straight back to the surgery.

The car park was almost clear, with just the Range Rover parked in the drive and Nigel's Volvo beside it. Surgery was obviously over.

She hurried in, her step so light that she felt she was treading air. But when she walked into Reception she stopped dead. The small group of receptionists looked up from where they were gathered, their faces shocked.

Gill beckoned Frances over and whispered in a low voice, 'Dr Quillan's had bad news. His son has been involved in a boating accident. They think the craft went down somewhere in Southampton Water.'

CHAPTER ELEVEN

Gill's words seemed to coincide with the door of Bruno's room flying open and Nigel appearing. Without hesitating, he strode across Reception towards them. 'Frances, could you pop in for a moment?'

The fact that the older doctor had said this in front of the staff barely registered, and she hurried into the room, her heart pounding. Bruno was dragging on a sports jacket and he swirled around as she entered.

She went to him. Instinctively they were in one another's arms. He kissed her on the forehead. 'You heard?'

She nodded.

'All three of them have been recovered from the sea. They were rescued by another boat and taken to Southampton General.'

'You're driving up there now?'

'Yes. Nigel's sorting out my calls for me. I haven't phoned Rosa yet. I'll leave it until I know more.'

'I'll come with you.'

He smiled and touched her cheek. 'No, I couldn't impose.'

'And I can't stay here waiting and wondering. That would be torture.'

She got her way in the end, and after a hurried change of clothes they set out

232

for Southampton. The journey to the hospital seemed to be one long blur of tense apprehension; nothing she could think of to say seemed worth saying.

'I should have made time to go with him,' Bruno muttered as they strode down the polished hospital corridor which led to the children's ward. 'I should have been there.'

Frances slipped her hand into his. 'I'm sure Christina and Nigel knew what they were doing. Stop blaming yourself, darling. It was an accident, that's all.'

He leaned against the wall, passing a hand across his face. Eventually he nodded. 'I love you,' he whispered softly. 'Thank you for being here for me.'

Christina, a small, dark woman in her mid-thirties, was sitting with Jack—two slight figures swathed in hospital dressing gowns perched on a bed. Somehow everyone was hugging each other as they linked together in an embrace.

When they'd recovered their breath, Christina told them how a charter boat full of holidaymakers had hit them and they'd been thrown into the water. She smiled proudly at Jack. 'Nigel had a bang on the head. We had to keep pulling him back to the boat. Luckily we were fully kitted out with jackets, but I should never have managed to hold onto Nigel without Jack's help. He was very brave.'

'And how's Nigel?' Bruno asked as he

233

wrapped an arm around his son.

She glanced at the overhead clock. 'He's having to stay put for a while, poor darling. Men's Surgical had a bed spare.'

'I'll show you the way.' Jack slid off the bed. 'I'm getting bored just sitting around.'

Bruno grinned 'Come on, then.' He glanced at Frances. 'Won't be long.'

When they had gone Christina sat back and sighed. 'It's so nice to meet you, Frances. Jack hasn't stopped talking about you.'

Frances smiled. 'All good things, I hope.'

'Very. He has great plans for you and Bru.'

Frances blushed. 'Has he? I . . . didn't realise.'

Christina hesitated. 'We're so happy someone special has come into Bruno's life.' She paused again. 'When Lindsay left him he was devastated. She was my sister and I loved her, but she treated him so badly and he didn't deserve it.'

Frances recalled his reaction over the Bally case, and though she had put it to the back of her mind, it still disturbed her. As much as he said he loved her, he had still confused her motives with Lindsay's. Lindsay had been such a powerful presence in his life, for good and for bad. Would he ever be able to truly forget her?

Finally, when Bruno came back, she realised that she was trembling. Although talking with Christina should have boosted her morale, somehow it had only helped to crystallise her fears.

She was hardly aware of what passed then—just of Christina bending to kiss her on the cheek before she left to go to her husband. Then Bruno occupied her seat and slipped his warm palm over her clenched fingers. 'OK, darling?'

She nodded. 'Fine.'

But she wasn't. She felt as though she were living in someone's shadow, no matter which way she turned. And she was beginning to think, even though she loved him deeply, that there was no resolution to the problem.

*   *   *

As Jack was kept in overnight they stayed in Southampton, booking into a hotel in the city centre.

'Thank you for being with me today,' Bruno whispered as they curled in the unfamiliar bed together. She felt his heartbeat under her hand, strong and regular. 'I asked Christina to come to Cerne Carey with Nigel for a few days' rest. But she's insistent she wants to get back to work.' He kissed her. 'Oh, my darling, I want it always to be like this for us—always.'

She put her fingers over his lips. 'Shh Sleep now. You're exhausted.'

He seemed to relax beside her. She closed her eyes.

'Darling, you're shivering.'

'N-no.'

'Let me warm you.' He pulled her into his arms and began making love to her.

He buried his face in her hair as he held her. 'I love your hair . . . it reminds me . . . Oh, God, you're such a beautiful woman.'

Don't! she cried silently. Please don't hurt me any more. Why did she have to look like Lindsay? It was so unfair!

And then, as he kissed her and began to replace her pain with the primeval instinct for making love, her desire for him engulfed her and she felt his body beneath her palms. In the agony of her love she forgot who she was, and who he thought she was, and knew just that she needed him one more time.

One more time.

Like an addict . . . Her addiction was love. The only way she would recover was to let him go. And in her heart she knew when that would be. In the autumn she would return to London.

*　　　*　　　*

Three weeks later there was an emergency call to Gabriel Bally's house at four o'clock in the morning. Frances walked into the surgery and came face to face with a haggard Bruno.

'Have you a minute?' He wore a blue sweater with no shirt beneath and a pair of

236

joggers.

She followed him into his room and he closed the door. 'Frances, Gabriel Bally suffered a massive coronary thrombosis in the early hours. There was nothing I could do . . . nothing. He had died at least an hour before I arrived.'

'Oh, Bruno . . . I'm sorry.'

He sat down behind his desk and rubbed his face with his hands. 'Petra Bally alerted us. In fact, she thought it was suicide.'

'Suicide!'

'She left him a week ago. She'd told him their marriage was over and he'd threatened to take his life. He called her, apparently, at midnight and he'd been drinking. She and the new boyfriend mulled it over for a bit and began to think he might do something silly. They went to check—eventually. When they found him she jumped to the conclusion that he'd probably overdosed.'

'But he hadn't?'

'No. All his medication from the hospital was unused. It seems he'd taken nothing since he'd been discharged.'

Frances sank into a chair. 'He didn't want to live without her.'

He shook his head. 'No.'

There was silence for a moment and she looked into his face, trying to read his thoughts. Had he, too, not wanted to live without Lindsay? A sense of desolation spread over her. Lindsay's ghost was always there. Since the boating accident she'd become almost paranoid that it was Lindsay who he was making love to, and slowly the knowledge was eating away at her. The more she thought about it, the more convinced she became.

'Is there anything I can do?' she asked softly.

'You can marry me, Frances . . .? Lord knows, in this profession we see too much unhappiness—our lives are so precious; I don't want to waste a moment more.'

She stood up, trying to remember how she was going to tell him. But she didn't have to. It was written in her eyes.

'For God's sake, Frances!' He stared at her disbelievingly. 'I thought . . . I thought it was just a matter of time—'

'Before I would say yes?' Her voice quavered. 'Haven't you taken into consideration what I may have wanted? Me— Frances Duncan! Pinch me, Bruno! Here!' She lifted her arm towards him. 'Look, I'm flesh and bone—I have a body which is mine, a mind, a thought process—an identity of my own! Can't you see who I am?' Anger and desperation had come to her aid now. She was saying what she had kept hidden in her heart all these months. Tears began to press against the backs of her eyes.

Anger spread across his face. 'Oh, for God's sake, Frances, are you telling me you still think

I'm confusing you with Lindsay?'

And suddenly her temper flared too. 'I believe you want what you couldn't have with Lindsay—not the future you could have with me.'

The arrow struck home. 'Frances, when is it going to sink in? I'm talking about us! Lindsay has nothing to do with us!'

She took a breath. 'I can't believe it. I wish I could, but I can't.'

He stared at her, his face frozen. 'Then there really doesn't appear to be much hope for us, does there?'

'Oh, Bruno . . . you said it yourself when you first saw me—you thought I was her. And that hasn't changed. She is still here— between us. One day you would wake up and find me, Frances Duncan, lying beside you and not Lindsay.' She choked back a sob. 'I just couldn't handle that.'

She looked into his eyes, praying that he would deny it. But he didn't. Instead, she fled from the room, certain now in the knowledge that he didn't love her. She wouldn't entrap him in a life that would one day become intolerable. She had been tempted, because she loved him. But love would not always be enough.

*　　　*　　　*

Harrington Hall's autumn term started late

this year, so Rosa told her. Jack was due to begin on the twentieth of September—a week away. For the last month she and Rosa had met either in Cerne Carey or at the flat, for obvious reasons.

This Sunday afternoon they were drinking in the coffee-shop. The news was good from Rosa's point of view. The accident seemed to have bolstered Jack's confidence. He had even agreed to go with Carl and play rugby that afternoon, much to everyone's surprise—mostly Bruno's.

'How is Bruno?' Frances made herself ask. She had barely seen him. The last few weeks she'd taken to phoning in to the surgery for any calls in the early mornings and then she'd slipped in when she was sure he would be out on calls.

'Miserable,' Rosa said bluntly. 'Frances, what happened?'

She shrugged and sipped her coffee. 'Rosa, it would never have worked. Bruno thinks he loves me, but I know he doesn't. It's Lindsay he's still involved with. I just have the unfortunate luck of looking like her.'

Rosa stared at her in astonishment. 'My dear girl, you've got it all wrong. If anything, your looks go against you. Don't you know that Bruno married Lindsay because she was pregnant?'

'Pregnant?'

Rosa nodded. 'I've never told Bruno, but my

daughter confided in me that she deliberately stopped taking the Pill.'

'Yes, but he must have loved her—'

'Frances, listen. Lindsay was my daughter and I thought the world of her—but I was well aware her tastes changed with the seasons. She was very much like her father. He died when she and Christina were very young. He was a restless soul and so was Lindsay. Christina, I believe, takes after me. We're homebirds—homemakers. Lindsay became bored and disenchanted with life very quickly. Whilst she was in training for a medical career Bruno fitted the bill, completed the image. But then she lost interest. Eventually the novelty of being a doctor's wife wore off. From the moment Jack was born she began to lose interest.'

Frances nodded. 'Yes, Bruno explained. But I can't convince myself he is over her.'

She shook her head sadly. 'Why do you think Bruno had the annexe built for me? Lindsay was never at home. Oh, she had her excuses, then, when Jack was three, she moved into the flat over her new venture—a design centre in Cerne Carey . . . I knew she had begun an affair. She said he was her business partner, but—' She shrugged.

'And Bruno knew too?'

'Oh, yes. By then he was well aware of Lindsay's mercurial nature. He was very fond of her, but when she took Jack away it was the

241

end.'

Frances felt suddenly desolate: Could she have been so wrong? Could she have turned him away because of her doubts and fears—not his?

'My son-in-law had only feelings of deep concern left,' Rosa elaborated as she seemed to connect to Frances's train of thought. 'He was worried for the instability of Lindsay's mind as Jack's mother. And then, when you came along, he told me he had found someone he could love and trust. But he had to think of Jack. He couldn't risk the child's peace of mind.' She smiled wryly. 'But, as you know, Jack had already made the decision for himself If Bruno was prepared to be cautious, Jack certainly wasn't. From the day you found him in Cerne Carey you were his friend.'

What Rosa said was true, she realised. 'Oh, Rosa, I just thought it was impossible to compete with Lindsay.'

'If you were anything like Lindsay, Bruno would never have fallen in love with you—of that you can be certain. And I should know. She was my daughter.' Rosa took her hand.

'Do you know that Bruno's decided to send Jack as a weekly boarder only, coming home at weekends?'

Frances shook her head. 'No, I didn't. Is Jack happier about that?'

Rosa nodded. 'Much. It's entirely due to you. Your influence on his father.'

Frances sighed. She was so confused. If what Rosa said was true, why hadn't Bruno contacted her? If he truly loved her, then surely he would have by now?

She looked up at Rosa. 'This is my last week—Benita is due to start back a month early . . .'

'Well, a lot can happen in a week,' she said, then asked softly, 'Do you love him?'

Frances nodded slowly.

'Then why don't you go and tell him?'

She was too afraid, was the simple answer. Too afraid to open herself out to love, to giving and receiving. Experience had taught her that she had never really loved Greg and that Greg had never really loved her. And now, when love had finally come along, she hadn't grasped it.

'It's too late, Rosa.'

'It's never too late.'

She cringed inside. She had harboured suspicions about Bruno—imagining him involved with Suzie Collins and Meg Fellows, only too willing to believe gossip—and then, when those had been proved untrue, she had accused a ghost! And all because she was afraid to let herself love, afraid of heartache. What must Bruno think of her?

She didn't deserve a second chance.

*   *   *

Nevertheless, she hoped that she might see him on Monday morning at the surgery. Not entirely sure of what she would say or do, as luck would have it, she missed him by inches as he left for his calls. On Tuesday he went to an accident mid-surgery, and she was busy on the Wednesday saying goodbye to her patients, preparing them for Benita's return.

Madjur and Serena gave her a beautiful silk scarf made in Delhi, since she'd admired their saris so much. Madjur was due to go in for joint replacements and promised that she would write to Frances in London and let her know how she fared. Little Freddie Clark's parting gift was a healthy gurgle of wind, and Sarah, free from her depression now, gave her a hug. Even Cynthia Vail said she would miss her.

On Thursday there was a small party in the office after surgery. Gill and the girls had brought wine and crisps and sausages on sticks. Each one of them, including Suzie Collins, bade her a warm goodbye. Nigel and Tristan popped in, and Meg too, and the general air of jokiness helped to cover her disappointment at not seeing Bruno.

On Friday, her last chance of seeing him, he was absent altogether. She crawled through the day, her heart so heavy that she felt like dying. She shed more than a few tears as she left the surgery at four and drove her last journey home to Bow Lane.

Praying for the phone to ring, she packed and tidied the flat, ready for the next tenant The phone was silent.

Before bed, she burst into tears again and sat in the bleak loneliness of the lounge. If ever there had been a fool, a self-centred, blind and stupid fool, it was her.

She was leaving the town she had grown to love.

And the man she loved.

What price her pride? She picked up the phone and dialled his home number. There was no reply.

Sunday's journey to London was as miserable as it could be. It rained all the way, in keeping with her mood. The Clio was packed to the brim. Not that she had brought much with her, but there seemed to be double going back. London was gloomy as only London could be on a wet Sunday. She nudged the Clio through the damp greyness and felt the fleeting uncertainty of the brooding loneliness of a big city.

The offer was there to go back to her old practice. Would she?

No, she had no desire to.

Soon the long rows of semi-detached houses which heralded her part of the world came into view through the swimming windscreen.

She was sick at heart. This was supposed to be home!

But home was where her heart was . . . down

in a little corner of Dorset.

She drew up at the small post-war building of modern flats at the end of her street. She could be on another planet for all she cared. She felt nothing. No familiarity. No warmth. No welcome. Tears filled her eyes as she looked down at her lap. They exploded over her lashes and dripped down onto her clenched hands.

The pain was terrible. But she had no one to blame except herself. All she could see was Bruno's lovely face, God help her. Now she was seeing him not only in her dreams but in broad daylight.

The knocking on the window made her jump. She blinked and shakily wound down the window. She was going crazy. Bruno was standing there—it *was* his face!

She reached out. Suddenly the door was open and he was pulling her into his arms.

She held on, sobbing, laughing, unbelieving. The rain bucketed down in torrents. They were standing there drenched, the water running in rivulets down their faces.

'But h-how . . .?' she stammered, licking the wetness from her lips.

'You left early!' His dear face with its dark lashes was shiny with rain. His dark eyes sparkled. 'I must have overtaken you somewhere on the road!'

She sobbed and swallowed. 'But I didn't see you! Oh, darling, why are you here?'

He threw back his head and laughed. And then he kissed her until she was gasping. 'That's why, you little fool!'

'But I thought I'd never see you again.'

The wind suddenly blew them against a drenched hedge and into another shower of water. They laughed and hugged and kissed.

'Did you think I'd let you go that easily?' he demanded, almost lifting her off her feet.

She shook her wet head. 'I didn't know what to think. Oh, Bruno—I tried to call you on Friday.'

'I had the day off. I took Jack and Rosa down to Corfe and the aquatic museum and then out to dinner. He's starting Harrington Hall tomorrow—remember?'

She groaned. 'I'd forgotten.'

'They missed you coming with us.'

'But I wasn't asked.'

'Would you have come?'

She hugged him for all she was worth. 'Oh, darling, of course I would.'

He peeled her away from him, blinking against the rain. 'Then we'd better get a move on. We can't waste his last night.'

'Do—do you mean . . . come back with you—now?'

'What do you think I mean?' He bent to kiss her slowly and deeply. Her hands travelled up to the dark, wet tangle of his hair and filtered through its thickness.

As they met each other's gaze little globules

of water bounced down from her nose and eyelashes. He kissed them away from her face. 'You're beautiful when you're wet.'

She laughed as he stroked the soaking strands from her face. 'It's getting to be a habit. Last time you lent me a sweater.'

'And this time—I give you my heart.'

She swallowed. 'Oh, Bruno.'

'I'm sorry I was such a fool . . . for keeping so much back . . . I was so afraid of losing you.'

'You'll never lose me. Not now. I'll never stop loving you.'

'Say it again,' he whispered.

'I love you, my darling. And I'll always love you . . . even if I do get pneumonia.'

He chuckled as he folded her into his chest. 'Don't worry, I know the perfect remedy. And the prescription lasts forever . . . Mrs Quillan . . . forever.'

Chivers Large Print Direct

If you have enjoyed this Large Print book and would like to build up your own collection of Large Print books and have them delivered direct to your door, please contact **Chivers Large Print Direct**.

Chivers Large Print Direct offers you a full service:

☆ **Created to support your local library**

☆ **Delivery direct to your door**

☆ **Easy-to-read type and attractively bound**

☆ **The very best authors**

☆ **Special low prices**

For further details either call Customer Services on 01225 443400 or write to us at

Chivers Large Print Direct
FREEPOST (BA 1686/1)
Bath
BA1 3QZ